JEALOUS BROADS

STILL ENVY

STEPHEN J BROWDER

PUBLISHER'S NOTE

Visit https://stephenjbrowder.wordpress.com or follow me on Facebook @ Stephen Browder to subscribe to my blog and receive updates on upcoming releases.

P.S

Be a pal and leave a review

BOOK I

CHAPTER 1

THREE YEARS AGO

"Now that you're staying here Seanna, I think it's important that we go over the ground rules. Just so you'll know what I'll be expecting from you," Roberta said before I could even get in the house all the way good.

I dropped my bags to the floor and said nothing.

"I know all about how you usedta do with your mama. But this ain't your mama's house and you can't do whateva you want to do up in here. You understand?" she continued with, obviously trying to get a reaction out of me.

Again, I kept my words to myself, knowing that there wasn't any point in trying to rationalize with this irrational woman. I had been down this road with her enough times to know that firsthand.

"You are to cook, clean, and do your part around here. One word of sass and I will literally slap the hell outta you. Try me if you wanna." She placed her hands on those massive hips of hers. Her eyes shone with challenge. I looked down towards my hands as nervousness began to get the best of me.

"I promise you that you won't get any trouble outta me, Ms. Roberta," I assured her in a tone that was barely above a whisper.

"Well, that's good to hear because I aint breeding no hoes up in here. I know you probably used to that and all being around your mama. But we don't roll like that around here. You understand me?"

I nodded my head in the affirmative, trying to stifle the feelings that were beginning to rouse in me from the ill way in which she spoke about the woman who had given me life.

Now, don't get me wrong, I realized that my mother wasn't a perfect woman by any means. If she was, she probably wouldn't be doing ten years in prison right now for identity theft. But a hoe, she was not, and I strongly resented the way that Roberta always tried to defame her name like that. Simply because she had been messing around with my daddy at the same time that she had been. If my mother was a hoe for that then what in the hell did that make her ass?

The Virgin Mary.

I let her finish her little spiel before grabbing my bags and heading to the back so that I could attempt to settle into this hell hole.

Roberta lived in a cramped, three-bedroom, stick-built home in Hollywood Hills, which was probably one of the roughest parts of Columbia and to say that I was thrilled about being here would be a flat-out lie. But this wasn't the only reason why I was so turned off by being here. In fact, it was dull in comparison to the realization that I would have to deal with her two daughters, who also lived here, on a day in and day out basis.

The thought was sickening.

Mishon, was her eldest daughter, whom everybody called Mish. She was 19. Three years older than me. The girl always appeared to have an attitude about something and didn't have many friends to speak of, which was probably why she always seemed to have something negative to say about anyone who crossed her path. She was tall and slim and had a lot of my daddy's features. The only thing that she seemed to pick up from her mom was her smooth dark skin. She really had a beautiful complexion, though I sensed that she was a little insecure about it with the way that she piled on the foundation, whenever she went anywhere.

Sakina, was Roberta's baby girl. Although, she was about a year and a half older than me. But I didn't count, of course, so that didn't even really matter anyway. Never have in this household. Everybody called her Kina for short. She had a little height, but not quite as much as her sister. Her and I were eye level at about 5'7. She was very curvy like her mama used to be before life began to get the better of her and it got out of hand. Where Mish was anti, Kina was a social butterfly and had a gang of friends as a result of her outspoken nature and her life seemed to center around their escapades. It must be nice to be in such high demand.

I could only imagine.

But neither of them seemed to care much for me and it was only because of who my father was.

It was stupid.

They acted like I asked to be their goddamn sister.

So fucking childish.

Roberta had already told me that Kina and I would be sharing a room, so I headed in that direction so that I could put away my things. The sounds of Drake's, In My Feelings, blared through the wireless speaker as I turned the knob and entered the room. Kina looked up from her laptop with a pissed off expression on her face, clearly annoyed about having her serenity deserved by the likes of me. I ignored her and walked over to the daybed on the other side of the room, which would now serve as my new sleeping quarters.

"Really. You gotta make all that noise just to come in the room?" she snapped, not even bothering to say hello or ask me how I've been doing, after what happened with my mama.

"What noise? All I did was open the door Kina. What are you talking about?" I asked in disbelief.

"You wouldn't get it," she said sarcastically. "I forgot who I was talking to."

"And what is that supposed to mean?"

Rather than to answer me, she simply put on her headphones and began messing around with her computer again.

Just plain rude.

I laid back and closed my eyes for a second in an attempt to relax, struggling to accept my new reality.

"Look who the cat done drug in from the suburbs. Miss bougie. I would like to welcome you to our humble abode," Mish said out of nowhere, mimicking the servant from, *Coming To America.*

Kina laughed like the idiot that she was.

So much for trying to relax.

"Hey Mish," I said meekly, not wanting to be taken off of my square.

"Sup," she responded with dryly. "Well, you mine's well get comfortable. Aint like you bout to be going nowhere, no time soon."

I said nothing to that. Just let her continue on.

"It's funny though," she said, almost right on cue.

"What's funny?" I wanted to know. Not finding a damn thing funny about this situation.

"It's funny how someone who always thought they were all that could be in a situation like you're in."

"Preach," Kina instigated, while waving her hand in the air like she was at church, summoning the Holy Spirit.

"Now that I think about it," she continued with, suddenly energized. "Both, you and your mama, thought that y'all were better than us. That's crazy. Now look at you, completely at our mercy. Eating our food. Sleeping in our bed."

"Nobody thought that they were better than nobody," I tried to explain before she cut me off.

"I'm still talking. Cut me off like that again and I will drag your bougie ass all up and through this house."

I looked up at her and saw that she was serious. Kina laughed as she saw the fearful expression that was on my face.

"Now that we have that understanding, I'll give you one word of advice if you want everything to go smoothly for you while you're here."

"And what is that Mish?" I asked in a voice that was barely above a whisper. A little afraid to hear the answer.

She bent down and looked me directly in the eye with a menacing smile on her face that revealed exactly what she thought of me.

As if there was any question about it.

"Stay the fuck outta my way. You heard. Do that and you might be all right, around here."

CHAPTER 2

PRESENT DAY

That was three years ago and I've been miserable ever since. But at least, at the early stages, I still had my father to turn to. But this last year has been really trying for me, ever since the accident.

Pops had just left Roberta's house. It was a pleasant day. Hell, even she had been in a good mood, which was very rare. He was crossing the intersection where Killian Road and Farrow Road met when he was T-boned by an eighteen-wheeler, killing him instantly. According to the coroner, he probably hadn't even known what had hit him. It had happened so fast. Pops had been drinking that day and had ran a red light, so his reaction time had probably been impaired tremendously.

At first, I had been mad at him for leaving me by myself like he had, knowing that he was my only ally in this whole world that could come through when I needed them to. But now that nearly a year has passed, all that I could feel was hurt. Mish and Kina had been devastated by his passing as well, but at least they still had their mother to lean on when they needed some consoling.

I had no one who I could turn to.

Well, I wouldn't exactly say no one because I have met someone who is quite special to me.

His name is, Tremaine Simeon.

He's a pro football player for Kansas City. This is his third year in the league and after much hard work, he made the All Pro Team for the first time this year, which was a major accomplishment. He was born and raised in Columbia, South Carolina and came back regularly to see his family and friends, which was how the two of us met.

I had just landed a job at Belk's in Sandhills and was in the men's apparel section hanging up some new inventory when I was suddenly interrupted by a tantalizing, male voice.

"Excuse me miss," he said while approaching me. "Sorry to disturb you. I just wanted your opinion on how you thought this shirt looked on me."

I was a little taken aback by how handsome that he was. Light brown with sharp, strong features. Neat dreads with blonde tips on them. Chink eyed. Juicy lips. He stood about 6'3 and his body was absolutely chiseled. The man probably didn't have an ounce of body fat to speak of. I pulled myself together and forced myself to be professional. I took a deep, relaxing breath then began to focus on the shirt.

It was one of the ugliest Polo shirts that I had ever seen in my life. Blue sleeves, red squiggly lines running across the front, stars that made me think about the fourth of July and Cinco De Mayo, all at the same damn time.

"You can't be serious right?" I asked him, seriously beginning to question his sanity.

"Yeah. So I take it you don't think much of it?"

Was this a serious question?

"No sir. I do not. Let me show you something that just came in today. I think it will suit you much better."

"Lead the way."

He followed me as I led him across the men's department to a tiny section in the corner, where we housed some of our edgier collections.

I took him to the Polo rack.

"There it is," I said more to myself than to him as I removed the shirt that I was looking for from the display. "Try this. You see how all the tones of blue just blend into each other."

He nodded his head to confirm that he did.

He smiled as he studied it.

"Yeah, this is hot."

"I believe this will suit you much better than that hideous thing that you were just over there, holding."

He laughed.

"I agree. I know your man must be the freshest brotha in town with you by his side, keeping him on point?"

I looked up at him to gauge what he was getting at.

"I don't have a man, but if I did, I would certainly do my part."

"I'm sure you would," he said with dancing eyes.

I was just about to walk away when he reached out and grabbed my hand.

"I'm sorry, where are my manners today? I don't think that I caught your name. I'm Tremaine by the way."

"Seanna." We shook hands.

"I see how you looking at me, Seanna. I'm not after nothing. I promise. I just wanna to see if I could get to know you better because you seem very interesting? That's all."

"But you don't even know me," I bluntly pointed out.

He smiled.

Now why did he have to keep doing that?

"I realize that, but I was hoping to get the opportunity to change all that," he said, without missing a beat with an all-too-serious expression on his face.

Everything within me told me to just walk away and let things be what they were, but something within told me that there was something different about this man.

I couldn't explain it.

But whatever it was, it was enough to influence me to do something that completely went against how I normally operated when it pertained to men who were trying to hit on me. Not only did I take Tremaine's number that day, but I also gave him mines and that night, when he called around eight like he promised to do, we talked for hours on end. We covered every topic imaginable and I nearly feel out of my seat once I found out that he was a professional athlete.

I didn't know how to feel about this.

I was 19 years old.

He was 23.

I was just getting out of high school and was working at Belk's until I figured out what I was going to do with my life. He was a pro football player with millions of fans around the world who rooted for him on Sundays.

He was the family hero.

I was the outcast.

We were as different as spinach and okra and here we were, actually considering being involved with each other, romantically. It was crazy.

I shared my thoughts with him, but he shut them down immediately. Not trying to hear any of it.

"We're not as different as you think Seanna," he explained. "The only difference is that I got an opportunity and made the most of it. But not everyone does. I'm grateful and realize just how lucky I am."

"That, you are," I agreed. "I don't know much about football, but maybe I will start checking you out on Sundays."

"You promise."

I laughed on my end of the line.

"Well, I can't do all that because I doubt if Kansas City games come on TV, every Sunday, here in South Carolina."

"You probably right. But my hope is that with this being the offseason and all, that by the time the season starts, we will be at a point where I can just fly you out to Kansas City to be by my side."

He was a very confident man and I liked that a lot.

"Who knows? Anything's possible, I guess. Why do I get the feeling that you've told this to a girl before?"

"Because you obviously don't know me like I want you to. I'm a genuine guy. God- fearing, and I don't play games with people's hearts. I just want you to see me for the man that I am and we can take things however slow you wanna take 'em baby. I wanna be someone who you can rely on with your life."

My heart fluttered in my chest from his powerful words and I realized in that moment, that it was fluttering because it was making room for Tremaine to establish residence.

CHAPTER 3

If it wasn't for the blessing of having Tremaine in my life, I probably would've went crazy by now. Living in this house with the three of them, took all of the resolve that I had within me sometimes, but by the grace of God, I just kept on keeping on, despite the challenge of the task. Every time that I called myself getting comfortable around here, something would happen that would let me know that this wasn't the place for me and it's been like this for the three years that I have been in this house.

Mish tried to bully me every chance that she got. Whether it was making me move from a seat at the kitchen table because she wanted to sit in it all of a sudden or taking forever to come out of the bathroom, knowing that I was waiting on her so that I could use it, it was always something and she was really beginning to get under my skin and she knew it to.

I did all that I could not to feed into her pettiness, but a girl could only take so much.

Being the adult in the household, you would think that Roberta would've done something to keep the peace when it came to the children, but she did nothing.

"Y'all go in the back with all of that shit," was the most that you would get out of her when her daughters where showing out. Unless it was me, of course. Then it was the end of the world, all of a sudden. Sometimes, I honestly felt like she wanted to see her daughters give me hell.

It wasn't a secret that she didn't care much for me. Never have. The only reason why I had been around this long was so she could make herself look like some type of outstanding woman for taking care of me, after my father passed. I wasn't a fool. Plus, I paid the light bill now so that was extra incentive to keep me around. Mish and Kina were both working just like me, but weren't asked to pay anything by Roberta, which just further showed me what she thought of me.

Getting out of this house was my top priority.

To show you what type of woman that she was, I'll take you back to last year.

- -

It was a week after my eighteenth birthday and I had less than a week before I graduated from high school, so I was pretty excited during this time. We were having dinner when Roberta's boss, Mr. Charlie had arrived. I hated when Mr. Charlie came over because I didn't like the way that he looked at me but up until this point, he had never said anything out of the way. But all of that changed on this evening.

I had on a tight pair of boy shorts. The one's that I slept in on most occasions. When he had arrived, I hadn't had a chance to change, due to the fact that none of us knew that he was coming over in the first place. Roberta usually let us know beforehand. That way, we could straighten the place up a bit before he arrived. But this time, she hadn't told us anything. Therefore, I hadn't had any time to change.

He stared at me like a hungry wolf as I crossed the room and headed to the table where he was already seated at.

Kina grinned in amusement as she saw the expression that was on my face.

I bet it wouldn't be so funny had it been her ass that this old, perverted white man was gawking at like this.

Mish didn't seem to care one way or another.

They both were a couple of jackasses as far as I was concerned.

"Hello there Seanna. How's my favorite gal?" he greeted, looking like one of the hyenas from, *The Lion King*.

"Hi, Mr. Charlie. I'm very well. Thank you," I said nothing more as I resumed eating my dinner.

"Have a seat Mr. Charlie," Roberta instructed with a fake smile on her face. "I'll run to the back and fix you a plate."

"Go on then," he told her with the dismissive wave of a hand. She quickly scurried to the back, like the modern-day, house nigga that she was.

To my surprise, he didn't sit at his usual place at the head of the table. He sat in the seat directly next to mines.

My heart instantly began to pound in my chest. I quickly woofed my food down and was finished by the time that Roberta returned back with his plate.

Mish and Kina had already finished as well and had made their way to the back. Like me, they didn't really care for being in the old man's presence and always got missing, whenever the opportunity presented itself.

I rose up to join them in the back.

"Leaving so soon, darling?" Mr. Charlie asked while winking his eye at me seductively.

"Yessir. I have some homework to finish before I go to bed." It was my last week of high school, so I figured that this would be a good excuse to leave, if any.

"What kind of homework do you have missy?"

"American History," I mumbled as Roberta took a seat directly across from me. She said nothing as the old man spoke, making me seriously wonder why she was even around in the first place.

"I was always very strong in history when I was in school," he informed me. "Maybe I can come back there and help you out with that."

"No, I should be all right," I told him quickly. Grossed out by the idea of being left alone with this creepy, old man.

"Seanna, if Mr. Charlie wants to help you out with your studies, let him. Ain't like you bringing home straight A's or nothing. You need all the help that you can get," Roberta scolded me.

I stared at her in disbelief.

"It's no problem really, honey," he told me, all too eagerly.

Much to my dismay, he followed me to my bedroom. Roberta led the way and dismissed Kina, who stared at me with a mixture of sympathy and amusement in her eyes, as she exited the room that we shared. I hated them. I hated all of them, and it was painfully obvious that the feeling was mutual.

I wasn't even a full ten minutes into my studies before Mr. Charlie reached out and began fondling my breasts. I asked him to quit, but there wasn't any stopping him. He slid his hand down into my shorts, despite my protests, and began massaging my vagina. I pushed him off me. Now horny and irrational, he came after me again. But this time, with a bit more aggression.

He wrapped his arms around me and attempted to slide my shorts off, but I wasn't having any of it. I kneed him in his nuts with all the strength that I had within me, sending him tumbling to the floor. He hollered out in pain, sounding like a wounded wolf. Roberta busted in the room in alarm with Kina in toe. Together, they stared in amazement, as they looked down at Mr. Charlie, who was now writhing around on the floor, balled up into a fetal position, clutching at his injured jewels.

Served his ass right, I remembered thinking at the time while mentally applauding myself for the amazing work that I had done to this child molester.

But my celebration was to be short-lived because once he got himself back together, he retaliated by promptly firing Roberta on the spot, leaving an atmosphere of doom and hopelessness behind as he made his exit in a hissy fit.

Roberta blamed me for getting fired, and so did Mish and Kina. I guess, it didn't matter to any of them that I had nearly gotten raped by a creepy old man. No, that part was unimportant. The only thing that mattered was that their mother no longer had a job and as far as they were all concerned, I was completely responsible for that happening.

Maybe, I would have been better off had I sat there and allowed the man to have his way with me. For some reason, they were never pleased with anything that I did around here. Somehow, I was always at fault, whether it was morally-correct or not.

CHAPTER 4

TREMAINE

Now, that training camp was over, I had a week of freedom before the regular season started and I intended on spending every second that I could, around Seanna. She was an amazing woman. An amazing person in general, and she had been through so much shit that it pissed me off, every time that I thought about it.

Not to toot my own horn, but I'm a dude who has never had any problems when it came to pulling a beautiful women. Once I got a little status about myself, on top of my natural abilities, it really wasn't a problem for me to pull a dime piece. But Seanna just sparked something within me, in a way that I really couldn't explain.

She was just as beautiful as any woman that I ever been with. Light-brown with gorgeous hair that she wore in a layered bob. Pouty lips. High cheekbones that dignified her. She wasn't super-thick like some of the video models that I've run across in my time, but she had a pretty body that complimented her perfectly. Her voice was light as a feather and made me think dirty thoughts whenever she whispered anything to me. She had it going on, but what I respected the most about her was that there was so much more going on with her than just the physical things.

She was humble in a way that was very rare for attractive women nowadays. I suppose it was a by product of the type of upbringing that she had. Whatever it was, I loved the way that she didn't seem to be so overtly impressed by the things that I had to offer, even though she didn't have much herself. It was almost as if the material shit didn't move her one way or the other and that was important to me because I didn't want to be with anyone who was with me for that reason. Like some of the gold diggers that I've been unfortunate enough to run across, in the past.

I called her the second that my flight touched down in Columbia and took her out for a night on the town. The two months that I had been away from her, felt more like two years and I didn't like the feeling at all. She blushed when I told her exactly how I felt about that situation, admitting that it had been rough on her as well, which gave me a warm, bubbly feeling inside. We did a little dancing and just basically enjoyed being in each other's presence again, after being apart for so long. She had on a blue, form-fitting dress that looked absolutely stunning on her. I told her that she was the most beautiful woman that I had ever saw in my life, meaning every word of it, as I escorted her to her seat at the Italian bistro that we were in.

"Yeah, right," she said skeptically while looking down towards her hands, obviously thinking that I was just talking for the sake of talking.

"I mean it, Seanna." I couldn't for the life of me, figure out why she didn't believe me.

"With all of the women that you've been around. Models, actresses, singers, strippers. I'm supposed to believe that you see me as being more beautiful than all of them. That's very hard to believe." She rolled her eyes playfully and smiled, obviously not taking me seriously.

"Yes, you are supposed to believe me because it's the absolute truth and if you give me an opportunity, I'll show you just how serious that I am about what I'm telling you." I looked her right in the eye, as I said that.

"And how exactly do you plan on doing that sir. I'm eager to know."

I now had her full attention, which was exactly what I needed right now.

"Like this," I said while pushing my chair from under me and grabbing her hand. She watched in shock as I grabbed her left hand and dropped down to one knee, right there in the middle of the restaurant.

"Wha-what are you doing Tremaine?" she whispered, as if in a trance.

"Since the day that I met you Seanna, I've felt like my life has finally gotten a sense of purpose and I realize that I feel that way because when I'm with you, I finally feel complete. I'm absolutely miserable when I'm not around you. Football's not as important anymore. Neither is anything that doesn't involve you," I paused so that I could get my thoughts in order before pushing forward. "I realize that you've been through a lot of disappointment in your life. A lot of pain, and I want to do everything in my power to keep you from having to go through any of that again because that's just how much that I love you baby. So, as I kneel before you, humble and willing, blessed to be worthy of a woman like you, I ask you Seanna

Nicole Traylor to take my hand in marriage and be my lawfully wedded wife."

Her jaw dropped to the floor as I reached in my pocket and removed the three-carat solitaire that I had picked up for her last week. Everybody in the restaurant were now staring at us with huge grins on their faces. A few pulled out phones and began recording the event, obviously recognizing who I was.

Up until this point, we had managed to go undetected.

Seanna cried and looked at me with so much love and trust in her eyes that it made my heart hurt. Damn, she had been through so much bullshit in her young life that it would probably be hard for her to ever trust anyone again. You could see it in her eyes. But despite all that, she decided to take another chance with me and I wouldn't let her down.

Ever.

"Yes, Tremaine. I would love to be your wife. Yes, Tremaine. Yes, Tremaine," she repeated in near hysteria.

I reached out and took her face in my hands and kissed her so tenderly that she basically melted against me as I pulled my lips away from hers. I settled our bill and quickly left the restaurant, happier than I had ever been in my life, feeling like

King Kong, with my wife-to-be so comfortably nestled beside me.

CHAPTER 5

SEANNA

It seemed like the moment that Mish and Kina had gotten news about Tremaine and I's engagement, they began throwing shade, and you didn't have to be a genius to figure out that it was out of pure jealousy.

The only person who seemed to be genuine happy for me was my friend, Alexis.

We had met when I first moved into Roberta's house. She had stayed over with two other girls for one of Kina's sleepovers and just like with any other sleepover that she had, I became their source of entertainment by making me the butt of their jokes. It never seemed to fail. Being new to the school, Alexis didn't particularly care for the way that they were treating me and came to my defense instead. The other girls turned against her instantly, but she didn't seem to care one way or another and I loved her for that. It wasn't long before we started hanging out and we have been tight ever since.

She was, in fact, the person that I turned to with all my troubles. No matter what she had going on, she was never too busy when I reached out to her. Alexis was amazing on so many levels.

She picked up on the second ring.

"What's up girlie? I was wondering when I was gonna hear back from your butt. I called you last week and never heard nothing back from your fat head," she scolded with that squeaky, high-pitched voice of hers. The way that she always did when a week or so passed without us talking to each other. I normally gave her a hard time about it too when she was the responsible party, so I really couldn't talk now, since I was the one to blame.

"Yeah girl, I meant to do it yesterday when Tremaine dropped me off, but you know all about how much drama be going on around here, almost all the time."

She said nothing in response, as she silently brewed over the way that I constantly got mistreated by Roberta and her two daughters. Alexis despised it so much that she no longer came to Roberta's house to hang with me anymore. For that was just how much that she was disgusted by it.

"So, how is my favorite couple holding up?" she said, changing the subject. "You know I love seeing the two of you together, don't you?" She was the only person in the world who I sincerely believed when they told me something like this.

"Tremaine is all that I could ever ask for in a man Alexis. I swear," I told her honestly, not wanting to brag too much, due to the fact, that my friend hadn't found her special-someone yet, which made absolutely no sense to me because she was so damn pretty. Light-skinned with green eyes. Tall and slim like a ballerina. Hazel eyes. Hair flowing down her back.

Now don't get me wrong, dudes lined up at the door for her. But she was very particular and so far, no one had been able to measure up to her standards and she wasn't the one to settle.

That was why she was so damn special. She knew her worth and conducted herself that way, whether anyone agreed with it or not.

"He treats me like I'm royalty or something," I continued with. "Not that I need all that or anything, but I'd be lying if I said that it didn't feel amazing because it does. I'm not really used to being treated this way as you very well know."

Again, her end of the line went silent.

A moment later, she decided to share a thought.

"Well, I'm glad a dude as good as Tremaine was able to come along and treat you the way that you deserve to be treated, Seanna. You are such a good person and I'm pretty sure that he feels as blessed to be with you as you are with him. Trust what I tell you."

Her sweet words caused my eyes to mist up a bit.

"You are such a big cry baby," she picked at me on her end of the line, knowing me too damn well.

"Whatever trick," I said defensively while wiping the tears away from my eyes, as if she could actually see them through the phone. "You be crying like a mug too. While you sitting there, tryna front like I don't know how you get down."

"I do not be crying," she lied. "My allergies just be bothering me sometimes."

Together, we laughed in amusement.

I decided to share some of my concerns with her.

"Alexis, let me ask you something?"

Hearing the seriousness that was suddenly in my voice, she stopped laughing on her end of the line and piped down.

"Yeah girl. Anything. What you got?"

She was all ears.

"It seems like no matter what I try to do that Mish and Kina always try to somehow pull me down. As if they don't want me to succeed in anything in life. Do you think they will ever let up on me? Because I seriously don't know." I had been thinking about this a lot lately and I needed her feedback on it because I continued to draw blanks.

"To be honest with you girl, I don't think they will. Not as long as you're around them. You might have to put some distance between y'all. You know, get away from all the drama."

She had been urging me to do so for quite some time now and finally, she was about to get her way.

It was time to share the big news with her.

"Guess what chicken head." I tried to keep the excitement out of my voice, but somehow, she picked up on it anyhow. Like she always did because she knew me so well.

"What's up hooker?" she asked breathily, obviously anticipating big news.

"Tremaine and I have gotten engaged." I squealed on my end of the line, as if just hearing the news for the first time myself because that was the first time that I had actually said it out loud to someone, since it happened.

"You lying?" she asked in disbelief.

"No ma'am. I shit you not. I'm flying out to Kansas City next week and then we'll figure out where we're gonna settle from there."

"Congratulations girl!" she sniffed as her emotions began to get the best of her.

She was such a little softy, for as hard as she liked to pretend that she was.

"I'm so damn happy for you and it couldn't have happened to a better person either. Just don't forget about us l'il people while you're living the good life."

Now, she should know me better than that and I told her as much.

"I'm just saying girl," she relented. "Hell, I might wanna come hang out with y'all in Kansas City one day and get my swerve on."

I laughed.

"Ain't nobody said we was even moving to Kansas City. We haven't decided on that part yet. There you go, jumping the gun."

"Well, I'm just saying girl. Wherever you end up, you just make sure that you stay in touch with me. That's all I'm saying."

"Alexis, you are my sister, girl. The only person, besides my husband-to-be who I know that I can trust out here. You've always had my back, when I had no one to turn to and I will forever love and cherish you for that. We will always be in touch heifer. You can't get rid of me that easily."

We both held the phone in silence and sobbed tears of happiness before it became too much for me and I ended our conversation.

You really couldn't ask for a better friend than Alexis and I swore that I would do something really amazing for her one day to show her how much that I appreciated her for always being there for me the way that she had. That day would come. For now, I just wanted to focus on being the best wife that I could be. Not that I had anyone in my life to learn this from. I would just have to figure it out on my own and hopefully, become a better woman for it.

CHAPTER 6

TREMAINE

The season was now officially over, and I had over a month to relax and indulge myself before I had to worry about conditioning, OTA's, and training camp. This was usually a time when I liked to reflect on the season that passed. Studied tape. Pinpointed the things that I felt like I had excelled in throughout the course of the year and more importantly, identified the things that I felt like had some room for improvement. That was the only way to keep getting better at what you did. Through self-critique because after all, you were the only one who knew your limitations, so it was you who knew what you were capable of and what you weren't more than anyone else could tell you.

This year we had finally reached the playoffs, after a seven-year drought, but had gotten dismantled in the first round. That was unacceptable and I looked to change that next year.

Had this been any other point in my life, I would probably be feeling pretty damn low right about now because that was just how badly that I wanted to win a championship. It was in my DNA because I had always been a winner. State champ in high school. National champ in college. But I have yet to reach the precipice in the pro game and that was simply unacceptable to me. Whether, I had only been in the league for three years or not. That was unimportant to me. In my eyes, we had a job to go out there and do and we had failed miserably in that regard or else, we would've reached the promised land.

Again, I looked to change that next year.

The only reason why I wasn't in the slumps right now was because Seanna was here. That always somehow, made everything not as important to me. When she was around, the only thing that really mattered to me was her.

It was time for us to start getting things in order so that we could prepare for our wonderful life together, and that would be a definite process. But I was excited about it.

So was Seanna.

The first thing that we had to decide on was where our primary residence would be located. I had no preference but would love it if she wasn't too far away from me because that would give me a little peace of mind knowing that I was always within striking distance, in case something went down while I was at the facility or something. We didn't have to necessarily stay in Kansas City because I was going into a contact year, next season, and with the amount of production that I've been able to put out since I came into the league three years ago, the chances of me returning with the team were slim to none. So, there really wasn't any telling where we would end up settling next.

The life of an athlete.

It wasn't that Kansas City wouldn't make me a decent offer because I was sure that they would. It was just that I would be demanding top-of-the-market money and they simply didn't have the resources available to them, due to other massive contracts that they were nurturing, to seriously compete with other interested teams.

However, it went, I would be cool with it. This was the business side of things and you just simply had to be ready when your number was called. Whether you had to clean out your locker or not.

For now, I would just do my best to give the good folks of Kansas City something exciting to cheer for because they were some of the best fans on the planet and they deserved nothing less than that. If I got traded next year, which was a very real possibility, I would go about my usual business, just like I always did whenever I stepped foot on the field. But I'd be lying if I said that I wouldn't miss this place if I left. Hell, this was the city that choose me over about three hundred other talented prospects when they could've just as easily have passed me up for someone different.

How could you not be appreciative of something like that?

So, if Seanna chose to stay put and settle right here in Kansas City, I would be just fine with that as well. I had love for the city and the city had always shown love to me, so I could very easily see myself calling this place home. But that was strictly up to my lady and I told her as much, during dinner, on the night that she came to town.

We had just gotten through eating our meal.

Some Kansas City-style ribs that we had picked up from one of my favorite barbeque joints in the city.

Seanna had been a little jet-lagged from her flight and didn't really feel like sitting in a restaurant at the time, so we had grabbed a meal to go. She really enjoyed the ribs and raved on and on about it until I switched up the conversation and asked her if she had come to a decision yet about where we were going to live.

"To tell you the truth Tremaine, I don't see why we can't just find a nice home right here in Kansas City. After all, this is where you spend most of your time and this way, we would be able to see each other a lot more than we have been." Noticing the strange way that I was looking at her, she smiled nervously. "You know. Well, at least, that's the way that I see it. But that's only if that's cool with you? I don't wanna interfere with your lifestyle, just because I'm here now and we're engaged."

"There you go, stressing over nothing again," I pointed out for the umpteenth time. She had a bad habit of retracting statements when she thought that it might be unsettling to someone and I was trying to get her to stop doing this. Sometimes, people weren't going to like the things that you had to say to them, and it was just that simple. I wanted her to come to terms with this reality and quit trying to please everyone.

The only person who she needed to be concerned about pleasing, other than herself, was me.

"Okay, okay," she said guiltily, realizing that she was doing it again. "I just don't want you to feel like you gotta switch up things. Just because I'm around. I want you to be happy too."

"Don't I look happy?" I asked through a huge, shit-eating grin.

"I guess." She laughed at my silliness. "If that's what you call that crazy look that you got on your face right now."

"I do," I said while smiling again. "So, it's settled then. We'll stay right here in Kansas City. I'll get my realtor on it tomorrow. Y'all can meet up and you can tell him what type of place that you have in mind."

She looked up at me with wonder in her eyes and I just had to know what she had on her mind.

"Everything okay bae?" I asked with concern as I tried to gauge her suddenly different demeanor.

"Yeah," she whispered. "It's just that you're so good to me Tremaine and I just can't figure out what I've done to deserve to be treated this way."

Was she serious right now?

"What you've done?" I repeated incredulously. "How about make me happy and feel like I now have someone worthy to serve, besides myself and God? When we first met, it might appear like I had my act all the way together, but I didn't. In fact, the only thing that I could seem to focus on was football and hell, to be honest with you, I could've been doing a helluva lot better at that. I was just going through the motions. Partying all the time with teammates and groupies. I had no real friends to speak of and I damn shole nuff couldn't depend on not one of them. Most of the people who were around me, did so for recognition and clout. That is until you barged into my life and blew all of that up."

"I did not blow nothing up," she said in a sing-song voice through eyes laced with emotion.

I reached out and pulled her down onto my lap.

She straddled her legs around me.

"You blew my heart up. That's what you blew up."

She leaned down and gave me a passionate kiss. I reciprocated. Sucking on her lower lip a little as she pulled her face away from mines. Suddenly beside herself, she pulled a bold move and reached down into my pants and began to stroke me like a woman possessed. The move had taken me somewhat by surprise because she was normally so reserved, but I was soon so overcome by her soft hands that I could barely think straight.

David met Goliath by the time that she slid my throbbing penis over the top of my basketball shorts. She stared down at it in wonder as she beheld it for the first time. Up until this point, we had never been intimate, on this level. Never going pass second base. I had wanted to wait until she was ready for it because based on our conversations about sexual things, I realized that she wasn't quite as seasoned as I was. Well, at least, that was my estimation, up until this point.

I watched in awe as she began to disrobe. She shifted around nervously as her own personal insecurities began to make their way to the surface. I quickly set her mind at ease.

"You are so damn beautiful baby. Please let me see all of you?" I groveled as I eyeballed her flawless skin and perfect curves.

Seeing the way that I was looking at her, her own confidence began to rise. She responded by unfolding her arms, which she had been using to shield her bare breasts from my perverted eyes, and she stood before me and allowed me the privilege of taking everything in.

What a fucking beauty, I thought to myself as I reached out and laid her down, ever so gently, on the hand-woven rug that my coach's wife had given me when I had first gotten drafted to the team. She looked up at me with all the trust in the world in her eyes and if I questioned if she was ready for this, it was answered in that moment because I realized that she wanted this to happen, just as much as I did. That was enough to give me some peace of mind.

Heaven met Earth as I entered her for the first time. She winced in agony as I broke her skin, but I was careful to take my time with her. Grunts of pain were eventually replaced by moans of ecstasy as I slowly inched myself in and out of her womb. Her pussy was so tight that it felt like I was in the sweaty grips of a professional bodybuilder and I knew that the end was on the horizon, but I paced myself so that I could continue acclimating her body with mines and it seemed to be a seamless transition.

"Oh, my-fucking-God. I think-I'm bout-to cum!" Seanna yelled out of the blue. A moment later, I could feel her pulsating on my dick, and it proved to be far more than I was capable of handling.

"Me too!"

The next thing that I knew, we were shaking together as the fireworks ignited.

We held onto each other tightly as we relieved our burden.

Oxytocin was released in both of our brains and for as drained as we both were, euphoria was the mood that eventually prevailed.

Afterwards, we both were totally spent, barely having the energy to get up to take a shower but somehow, we managed, despite the amount of effort that it took. I gave Seanna a brief tour of the condo that was to be her new home. Temporarily, at least. Until we found a home that was more suitable to claim. She took it all in and seemed to be thoroughly impressed.

You ain't saw nothing yet, I thought to myself.

After loading her suitcases into her closet, I crashed onto the bed like a dead body. She followed suit, equally as exhausted as I. I reached out and pulled her closely to my chest. She nestled in and tightly clasped her arms around me.

I sniffed her hair as I drifted off to Never Never Land. It smelled like strawberries and had an unexpectantly soothing effect on me.

She told me that she loved me, and I told her that I loved her more. Meaning every word.

It felt good to have her next to me like this.

It felt really good.

I knew right then that I never wanted to let this feeling go and that I couldn't allow nothing, or no one, to come between us.

Ever.

Never did I think that the day would come that I would feel like this about anybody but, here, I was, and I didn't regret anything about it.

CHAPTER 7

SEANNA

My transition from Columbia to Kansas City went along about as seamless as a person could ever hope that it could, and I had Tremaine to thank for that. The man was constantly at my beck and call but was mindful enough to give me my space and allow me to figure things out for myself sometimes, which was something that I really respected about him. He didn't want me to lose sight of the person that I was.

It was so easy for a woman to lose her own identity when dealing with a man of Tremaine's caliber, with them not ever really having to worry about anything, anymore. *Bae, I need this. Bae, I need that.* That was why no matter what the circumstances were, you always had to maintain some sense of individuality or else, you may forget where he ended at and where you began.

I'm not knocking anyone who chooses to live this way, just for the record. But in life, you just never knew when you would be forced to step up to the plate and hold things down on your own and you had to be ready to face the challenge and not get too absorbed with living the good life that you become handicapped when such an occasion arises. Having money couldn't overcome every, single thing that you may come up against. That's why you always had to stay humble and prepared.

I still talked to Alexis on a regular, but that was about as far as my dealings with Columbia went. Mish and Kina could be on fire for all that I knew, and I wouldn't know a thing about it, unless Alexis told me about it herself. Maybe once they matured a little and stopped being so damn petty all the time, we could sit down like three grown women and repair our fractured relationship because we were sisters after all. Whether they wanted to accept that reality or not.

I hated that things stood the way that they did between us to be completely honest about it. It hurt me very much. But at the same time, it wasn't like I was the one who had shut them out. I was the recipient and refused to continue to be their victim, simply because they didn't like who my mama was.

Hell, I didn't like the woman at times myself.

It's been over three years since I've heard from her and honestly, it didn't even bother me no more. My mama had always been more about herself than she had ever been about me and I couldn't just pretend like it was all good anymore. Locked up or not, you could still reach out to your child, so I wasn't trying to hear any of her excuses whenever the day came that I did hear from her again because I knew how she was already.

I knew her better than anyone else did.

When I agreed to come out here and move to Kansas City with Tremaine, I must confess that the fact that he played for the team in this city was only a part of the reason why I agreed to find a home here. The other reason being that I wanted a place to have a fresh start at and for as nice of a city as Columbia is itself, I had too many negative memories associated with it to forge ahead in that environment. It could have been done, but it most definitely would've been more challenging and why create unnecessary problems for yourself, when you really didn't have to.

I had nothing to prove to anyone.

As it turned out, moving to Kansas City seemed to be just what the doctor ordered for me. I flourished in this town and everybody treated me like I was a celebrity.

The perks of being engaged to Tremaine Simeon.

And I thought that he was a big deal in Columbia with him being a native of the city.

In Kansas City, they honored him on a whole other level.

He was a god.

Just take the other day for instance.

We had just left the Arabia Steamboat Museum and were on our way to the Worlds of Fun Amusement Park when the local paparazzi ran up on us, snapping pictures, asking questions about who I was and what was our relationship status. According to one member of the press, we had been spotted around town, by various viable sources, and they wanted to know a little something about the mystery woman. Tremaine introduced me as his fiancé. I guess so that people would no longer have to question my importance in his life. It was only when they tried to push me for more personal information, did he shut them down completely.

"That's it, folks. As you can see, we are out here tryna enjoy ourselves and would really appreciate it if you all allowed us to do that in peace."

They backed off but continued to keep themselves in the general vicinity and after about another hour of dealing with this insanity, we just wanted to wrap it up and go back home.

As we made our way to the exit, a woman cut us off by stepping in front of us. Tremaine's head snapped in her direction and it was obvious that he was none too pleased by the rude, deliberate mood and I really hoped that he didn't make a scene out here. But my fears were to be short-lived because once he really got a good look at her, his expression softened, and it was obvious that he already knew her.

This should be interesting, I was pretty sure.

"Jordan," Tremaine greeted in a sing-song voice while reaching in and offering the woman a friendly hug. "How's everything been?"

"Well, as about as good as can be expected, I guess. The blog has now reached a national level and my morning talk radio show is really booming right now. I mean, really booming. With the way that things are going, I hope to put,

Wendy Williams, out of business by the end of the year," the woman said in what I hoped was dry humor because if she seriously thought that she was about to put Wendy Williams out of business, she had to be smoking something that killed braincells and commonsense.

I sized her up.

She was about the color of a brown paper bag and had beautiful skin. Stood about an inch or two taller than me, which put her at about 5'8. Her hair was about shoulder-length and she wore it naturally. She had deeply-slanted eyes that made me wonder is she possibly had any Asian descent in her bloodline. She was a bit on the frail side and didn't have many curves to speak of. But she was graceful and moved like a ballerina when she walked. She was the type of woman who you noticed when she entered the room, whether you were checking for her or not. The girl definitely had presence, if she didn't have anything else. But pound for pound, she couldn't hold a candle to me.

Not that we were in an actual competition or anything.

"Where's my manners, today?" Tremaine apologized before turning his attention back to me. *Hell, I was surprised that he even remembered that I existed with the way that he was going on and on with this woman.* "Jordan, this is my fiancé, Seanna Traylor. Seanna, I'd like for you to meet, Jordan St. Claire. She's one of the biggest radio show personalities in this entire city. Believe it or not."

"Well, I wouldn't say all that, but I do manage to make do with what I got to work with," She explained simply, putting on like she was humbler than she actually was. But I knew better than to fall for that charade because it was rather obvious to me.

"Nice to meet you," I said meekly, noticing the way that she was looking at me. "So, how do y'all two know each other?"

Tremaine smiled guiltily as he looked to Jordan.

"Well, that's a long story," was his half-assed explanation.

"When your fiancé first got drafted to the team, I covered him. He came down to the station for an interview, which is customary for all of the new budding superstars of our team," Jordan explained innocently but I sensed that there was more to come. "We sort of hit it off and things just pretty much went from there."

Went from there? What was she trying to imply?

I decided to get clarity.

"Meaning what exactly? What, did the two of you used to date or something?"

Tremaine smiled at me guiltily.

"Well, I wouldn't exactly say that we were dating as much as we were just hanging out. But I think that the two of us were both too preoccupied with our careers for it to become anything serious." Jordan shrugged as if it wasn't really a big deal, but I didn't brush it off so easily.

"Really. And do the two of you still remain in contact?" I asked while turning my attention back to my husband-to-be.

"Well bae, she's kinda hard to avoid because we're both public figures in the same city."

"Right," Jordan intervened. "But I wouldn't expect you to understand that because you strike me as the Susie-homemaker type, so you wouldn't know anything about that arena."

Seeing that she was starting to get under my skin, Tremaine dismissed her before our conversation could go on any further. Even though, I still had more questions, I decided not to drill her about it at this time.

Tremaine and I had plenty of time to talk more about her once we got back to the house.

CHAPTER 8

JORDAN

So, Tremaine has gone out and gotten himself a fiancé just like that. It has been less than a year since he and I parted ways and now, he was talking about marriage, and to a little ghetto ragamuffin like Seanna. No sir. It wasn't about to go down like that. What did he expect? For me to just sit around idle and allow him to play me out like this? He had me twisted, if that was what he was thinking.

This chick was weak, and I recognized that immediately. There was no way that I would've stood around like her, while my man shot the shit with some chick that I found out that he used to date, and not act like a plume fool up in that joint. So again, he had been brushing me off all this time, just to end up with the likes of her. I didn't think so. I mean, I realized that I didn't know the girl personally or anything, but it wasn't like it took a whole lot for me to be able to figure her out.

I knew her kind.

She was the type of chick who went along with anything that her man said or did, so long as he was feeding her and was showering her with lavish things. Really, no better than a pet, like a Pomeranian for instance. She had come from nothing in most likelihood and was just so glad to finally be out the projects that nothing else mattered to her, and Tremaine deserved so much better than this little welfare case could offer him.

He was smart, handsome, and focused on being the best player in the league, which meant that when it was all said and done, he would be a very powerful man. He needed a woman like me, who was equally as driven and accomplished in my own right, to compliment him and become the ultimate power couple.

Just like Russell Wilson and Ciara.

Since the chick wouldn't tell me nothing about herself that I could possibly use against her, I decided to do a little digging on my own and it proved to be much more challenging than I initially anticipated that it would be.

Not only did Seanna not have a Facebook account, but she wasn't on Instagram, or Pinterest either. But luckily, I was able to track her down on Twitter and I found out everything that I needed to know about her there.

I was a little surprised to find out that she was from Tremaine's hometown of Columbia, SC. She didn't have many friends or followers, less than one hundred people, and only had a few inspirational tweets on her timeline. Nothing personal for me to be able to get some feedback from. I searched up her family and friends and this was where I hit the jackpot.

Apparently, she had two sisters. A girl named, Mishon "Mish Mish" Traylor, and another who went by the handle of, Sakina "Chocolate Bunny" Traylor. I went to their pages and it didn't take me long to figure out the extent of their relationship with Seanna. They both slayed her, every opportunity that they got.

I smiled.

I wasn't a big twitter head, so I pulled up both of their profiles on Facebook instead and sent them both friend's requests. Mishon was the first to accept. Sakina accepted later that evening. I instantly jumped in Mishon's inbox.

I told her that I was a blog columnist and radio show host and that I was looking to do a story on Tremaine because he was one of the biggest names in our city. I then went on to explain that I was aware of his recent engagement to her sister and that I was having trouble learning her story and needed some feedback from someone who was close to her. She surprised me by the way that she responded to my request.

Obviously not the type to mess around, Mishon stated. "So, you need some dirt on her, pretty much?"

At first, I didn't know how to respond. But I knew that I had to tell her something or else, she may not help me out. So, I just told her through a private message that I needed some information about Seanna and that I wasn't on a specific mission to destroy or absolve her from any wrong doing. I told her that I just needed the facts and that was all.

She wasn't buying one word of it.

"Yeah, the fuck right," Mish typed back in obvious disbelief. "You want to destroy her, and I know that because if you didn't, you never would've contacted me and my sister. Didn't think that I knew about that, huh? Lol."

I said nothing in response.

Ten minutes later, she was back in my inbox. This time, with a proposition.

"Just so you know, I think somebody need to get her ass off her high horse and maybe you're the person to do it. I'll tell you whatever you want to know, but it's going to cost you."

I thought it over for a second before messaging back. "How much money are you talking about?"

She messaged me back immediately.

"I'll send you a Paypal request. What's your email address?"

CHAPTER 9

TREMAINE

It seems like ever since Seanna found out that Jordan and I used to date, that she has been acting kind of funny. Maybe it was just my imagination playing tricks on me because it wasn't like she was doing anything that different from what she had always done. She still came up to me and gave me a hug whenever I came back home from taking care of some business and she was still very much intimate with me, and it wasn't like she had suddenly gotten sly out of the mouth or anything as obvious as that.

It was more about the little things that she did.

The way that she looked at me when I told her about my day or the way that she responded when I called her and told her that I would be coming in late. It was sort of like she didn't trust me anymore and that bothered me a great deal. I suppose

I should've told her about my past involvement with Jordan, but it wasn't like I had been cheating on her so really, what was the big deal? I had never told her that she was the only woman in the world that I had ever been with or anything, so I couldn't figure out the reason for the sudden change within her.

She was tripping for no reason whatsoever and we most definitely needed to have a real discussion about that.

In order to do something productive, Seanna had started a non-profit organization that she was pretty energized about. She named it, Second Chance Academy. Her specialty was finding trades for troubled teenaged girls who had come up, primarily in foster care, so that they could have a brighter future. I had given her a quarter million dollars to fund this organization, which had been just enough for her to hire a counselor and link up with a few career centers in the state of Missouri, who would help turn her dreams into reality. The center was doing extremely well, much to my surprise, and I was proud of her for being so diligent about an issue that she was obviously so passionate about.

She had just gotten back in from work when I cornered her in the living room and asked her if she had something that she wanted to talk to me about.

"No, not really," was her simple response as she hung her keys on the coat hook by the door, like she always did.

"You sure because you certainly been acting like you got something that you need to say to me," I said, not willing to let her off the hook so easily this time around.

"From the sounds of it, you're the one who has something on your mind."

"As a matter of fact, I do," I told her honestly.

"Such as?" she asked while taking a seat on the couch.

I followed suit.

"Why is that you've been seeming so distrustful of me, lately? It's like you been moving different since that whole l'il thing with Jordan St. Claire came out, or am I mistaken?"

"Well, to be honest with you, I didn't like the way that everything came out at the amusement park. It was embarrassing and made me look like a dumb ass fool. Even if nothing really happened between you two. I still felt like you should've been open with me from the jump. That way, I could've been a little more prepared for this type of thing when it came up. But to be honest, I'm over that now. I have other things on my mind."

Noticing that she was looking stressed, I inquired about what exactly it was that seemed to be troubling her.

"You remember that girl, Tony Douglass, don't you?"

Tony was one of the young ladies whom Seanna had been working with. She had just gotten out of the juvenile detention center when they had met. She was a good girl but was noticeably scarred. Turns out that her dad had been raping her since she was 10 years old and she had retaliated by slicing his throat in his sleep the day after her 14th birthday. By the grace of God, the man had survived and promptly pressed charges on his daughter for nearly killing him, which got her sent to the juvenile center until she reached adulthood.

18 years old.

Seanna identified with this young woman immediately, based on her own harsh experiences and even started spending more one-on-one time with her to show her that she could trust her because she was truly her friend. She was a gorgeous little dark-skinned chocolate drop and it tore me up whenever I saw the two of them together and thought about everything that she had been through at such a tender age. But at least, she now had an ally in Seanna and let me tell you from personal experience, that she was most definitely a good ally to have.

"Yeah, I remember her. How could I forget?" I asked.

"Well, I just found out yesterday that she blew her own brains out in an alley. I knew that she had been going through some things, but never would I have imagined that it had gotten to this extent. How could I have missed that?"

Out of nowhere, she started bawling uncontrollably. I grabbed her tightly in my arms and tried to console her as best as I could, but it didn't seem to help. I had to wait until she was ready to calm down on her own, which took about ten more minutes to accomplish.

"I'm so sick of users and miserable people, preying on the innocent, until they damage so much within them that they don't have nothing left to fight with no more. It ain't right, I tell ya. It ain't right," she ranted more to herself than to me. She was starting to scare me with the way that she was carrying on, but I decided not to interrupt her as she continued to vent her frustrations.

"And once they see that they got you down, they continue to put their foot on your neck. Not caring about the way that it may be affecting you." She took a second to catch her breath and collect her thoughts.

"Some people don't even think about what they might be doing to the other person. They just be doing what they feel like doing, without even thinking about it," I added.

"No, I ain't buying that," Seanna said while looking me right in the eye. "They be knowing what they be doing. They not stupid. They just don't seem to give a fuck is all. But somebody has to fight back and put these lowlifes in their place. That's why I'm making a vow on this day. Anybody cross me, from this point forward, without probable cause, I'm gonna be the one to humble them. Mark my words on that one."

I said nothing, just simply stared at her, as I tried to figure out if she was just making a generalized statement or if her words were also directed towards me. *Was she threatening me?* I just couldn't seem to figure that part out. I started to question her on it but one look in her eyes told me that this clearly wasn't the time to be badgering her about anything.

She dismissed herself and sauntered away to the back so that she could bathe and get herself comfy. I watched after her as she left but stayed where I was at on the couch as I tried to organize some of the clutter that was consuming my mind. Maybe I had been mistaken about her sudden change in demeanor. Maybe she wasn't tripping over the Jordan thing at all and it was just me reading into it the wrong way. That was very possible. Maybe she had just reached her breaking point because she has in fact, been through a whole lot in life, and was starting to transform herself into someone who I would need to become better acquainted with.

I supported her one hundred percent as I've demonstrated to her time and time again. But I sincerely hoped that she didn't try to instill too much change on me, too soon, because I didn't do change like that.

Never have.

CHAPTER 10

SEANNA

The loss of Tony proved to be one of the toughest things that I've had to deal with up until this point, in my young adult life. Sometimes, life can be so unreasonable and unfair. Causing such a beautiful, vibrant young lady to endure so much, at no fault of her own. Leaving her so depressed and distraught over her circumstances that she felt no way out but to take her own life.

For as excited as I had been initially over my little non-profit organization, suddenly it became a burden on me. Going to Second Chance Academy no longer excited me because the only thing that it made me think about was Tony every time that I stepped in the building. It got so bad that I had to ask my co-founder Jessie to take over for me full time.

Understanding what I was going through, she accepted without even thinking twice about it.

I had decided to do something that would take my mind off everything. I went to the gym so that I could burn a little energy. Last month, I had decided to renew my membership because I had picked up a little extra weight and wasn't feeling it at all.

I normally wrapped up my routine by doing a little cardio and normally mixed it up between the treadmill and the elliptical. Today, I had decided to ride the treadmill mill for twenty minutes before calling it quits.

I plugged my headphones into the console and turned to a local radio station. They were talking on almost every station, so I ended up settling on 107.4, The Heatwave. I instantly recognized the voice as the woman on the station replied to a comment from her co-host about groupies preying on celebrities.

It was Jordan St. Claire.

"Well, I can't say that Bill Cosby was necessarily preyed on, if you ask me, because whether he did what he was accused of, to all of those women or not, doesn't negate the fact that he did, in fact, abuse some of the women who accused him. That is pretty much undeniable at this point," Jordan explained with a studious tone. "So, he deserves what he ended up getting as a result of his actions, plain and simple, because he put himself in that position, so he gets no sympathy from me. R Kelly's nasty, pedophile ass either. But there are a few others out here who I do sympathize with because I realize that they've been placed in certain situations unknowingly. That makes a difference to me." She finished with.

"I already know who you gonna say because we spoke about this issue last week, under a different segment," her co-host, TK Daniels, pointed out in what was an obvious lead up to whatever it was that she was about to say next.

"Yessir. I just don't know what some of these rappers and athletes be thinking, dealing with some of these women." Her tone was one of disapproval and disgust. "Just take Tremaine Simeon for instance. What in the world would possess him to deal with a criminal? I mean, you would think that a man of his caliber would be capable of meeting a woman who actually brought something to the table. Not one that stole people's identities for a living and then turned around and snitched on their own damn mama and got her thrown in the slammer for ten whole years. Come on now. I mean, just think. If a woman is willing to do that to the woman who birthed her then what in the hell did you expect her to do to your ass, if you were ever in a jam? Suddenly, become noble like Mother Teresa or something. I think not, sir."

TK laughed at her rhetoric, which only served to piss me off, even more than I was already.

I was so pissed off after hearing this nonsense that I stopped riding the treadmill but still, I kept my composure long enough to listen to the rest of the show.

"But how do we even know if that's true or not," TK added, which got a silent applause from me because at least, someone on the show had sense enough to question the source of the information.

"Because according to the good folks over at *Gossip Weekly*, her entire family corroborated the story. Including her mother, who is still serving time in prison for the egregious offense. Just read the article TK. It's all there, money."

Now, I really couldn't believe this shit.

"Well, if that's true then that's jacked up on some many levels. Brother better have an exit strategy in place. In case things hit the fan." They both laughed.

I didn't find a damn thing funny about any of it.

I went to the locker room to take a shower and was just about to go in when it hit me. I started crying. Then, I started yelling and punching the wall. Again, and again. I hit it so hard that my knuckles started to bleed, but I kept right on hitting it anyway, feeling virtually no pain. I don't know what had gotten into me. It was almost like I had stepped outside of myself and was in sort of an observation mode. A place where I could only watch the things that I was doing but was powerless to stop from actually happening. It was weird but empowering at the same damn time.

Someone had to pay.

It was time.

I laughed hysterically as I washed the blood off my hands and wrapped my right hand with the paper towels that I had just pulled out of the dispenser.

A scrawny white woman had walked in towards the end of my little episode. Seeing the fit that I had just thrown, she approached me and asked was everything okay and did I need any help.

"No, it's not okay," I told her honestly, staring at her with a serious expression on my face because I meant every word that I was saying to her. "But it's about to be okay." I laughed like a crazed maniac. "Yeah, it's definitely about to be okay."

Before she could ask me what I meant by what I had just said to her, I snatched my gym bag out of the locker and stormed out of the locker room, leaving her staring after me in utter shock and confusion.

CHAPTER 11

TREMAINE

I was livid once Seanna filled me in on the things that Jordan had said about her today on the air. The nerve of her, to go to such extremes to humiliate my woman. She was obviously hating on Seanna and I felt that at least, one person in the room should've been able to pick up on that immediately. But maybe, I was giving them too much credit.

There was one little problem though.

Jordan was connected and as far as the general public was concerned, she was credible, so when she spoke, people listened automatically because of the reputation that preceded her. Most of her listeners took the things that she said to the heart, which didn't help me and Seanna's cause at all.

Not one bit.

After hearing Seanna rant on and on about how foul and despicable that Jordan was, I decided to reach out to her myself. Maybe, closure was the thing that she needed to capture for her to just move on with her life. So, I decided to give her what she was seeking.

After making numerous attempts to contact her, I finally got through. She picked up on the third ring. I decided to get right down to it because there wasn't no need in dragging this out, any longer than I had to.

"I was calling you because we need to sit down and talk," I told her immediately without even bothering to greet her. "So, when are you free?"

She thought about it for a moment before responding.

"Your girl there?" she asked with caution.

I reluctantly told her that she wasn't.

"Good. Because I ain't tryna be throwing blows with nobody right now. I don't have the time for it." She laughed a little after making her comment.

I said nothing at all.

"So, what are you doing right now because I'm free, and you obviously have something on your mind that you need to discuss with me or else, you probably wouldn't have reached out to me like this."

Now, why was she playing dumb, acting like she didn't know what it was that I wanted to talk to her about.

Crazy ass woman.

That was why I'd had to stop dealing with her when I did.

I gave it some thought.

Seanna didn't get off until about 5:30. It was a quarter to 3:00 now. Plus, it wasn't like we would be talking for all that long, so we should have plenty of time to have our little conversation before my lady got in. That way, we could get this messy business behind us, once and for all.

"I'm free. Come through. You still remember where I live, don't you?" I instructed her.

Seanna and I have yet to find a new home and weren't even looking all that hard, to be completely honest about it. So as a result, we still stayed at the condo in which I've lived for the last few years. Jordan had been here a time or two herself, back when we used to mess around. Although, that had been a nice little minute ago, so I wasn't sure if she still remembered where I stayed.

"How could I forget?" she asked with much innuendo in her tone, bringing my uncertainty to an end.

I was starting to wonder if having her come to my place like this was such a good idea.

I brushed the thought aside and invited her over anyhow, figuring that I could handle whatever unexpected turn that may come my way.

Boy, was I so wrong about that.

The instant that Jordan stepped in the door, an uneasy feeling washed over me once I saw that she was wearing a trench coat and a pair of red pumps. She had come over to my place before sporting such attire and every time that she had, she never had on anything underneath it, save a flimsy bra and a tiny pair of panties. So, I knew exactly what it was that she had on her mind.

The nerve of this girl.

What if Seanna had been here? But wait, I had already told her that she wasn't here before she came, which had probably been her whole reason for asking in the first place.

"You wanted to see me?" she asked very seductively while dropping her trench coat to the floor, not even bothering to close the door behind her.

"What, are you crazy?" I asked in a panic as I scurried to the door and closed it behind her before any of my neighbors could see what was going on in here. That would be all that I needed right now. To make a spectacle of myself like this. She approached me the instant that I turned back in her direction. I tried to move away, but it was too late. She closed in on me and pinned me against the door.

"Do you ever be missing the times that we used to share with each other, Tre? I know I do. We used to have a lot of fun together. Don't you remember?" She pressed her body against mine and she was so damn soft. I asked her what she was doing. She responded by kissing on my neck. I asked again but this time, she reached down and began to rub my dick through my pants instead.

I reached down and pushed her hand away before it could go any further.

This girl had a lot of goddamn nerve, coming in here like this.

I wasn't even about to go out like the clown that she was trying to make me out into.

Not this nigga here.

I mean, don't get me wrong, she was a sexy little thing. Pretty as hell with legs that ran longer than the Great Mississippi River. There was no denying her physical appeal. But my woman was fine too, if not, even more so, and she brought so much more to the table, other than her looks. Jordan was right. We did used to have a lot of fun together, but it was dull in comparison to the fulfillment that I got when I was around my lady. Nothing else could possibly compare to that, so why even entertain it in the first place?

Jordan was the type of girl who you called up when you were ready to wild out and just wear somebody's ass out without having to deal with a whole lot of complication about it. She would top you off without even thinking twice and let you have your way with her in a way that would make the founders of Burger King cringe. There is a time in a young, athlete's life, when being surrounded by women of Jordan's caliber confirmed that you had, in fact, arrived. It showed the world that you were on a whole other level and you wore it like a badge of honor. But besides the boost to your already over-inflated ego, it really didn't accomplish much else.

It was good for men who needed that type of validation.

But women, like Seanna, were on an entirely different plateau.

Women like Seanna were the type of women who all the playboys of the world wished they had been able to get it together for and do right by, once they became old and washed up and looked back on their miserable, unfulfilled lives with deep regret.

I wasn't trying to be one of them.

Jordan was a thing of the past for me and I had no interest in her whatsoever. I was all about the future and Seanna was the only woman who I wanted to share it with.

I pushed her off me and reached down and grabbed her trench coat off the floor. She stared at me with a mixture of resentment and disappointment in her eyes as I shoved it back to her. It was obvious that she was a little heated about the fact that her plans hadn't gone the way that she had envisioned them going.

She was most definitely barking up the wrong tree with me.

Not this man here.

This man here belonged to Seanna.

I opened the door and told her to get the fuck out.

She shook her head, as if I was the biggest fool in the world for not taking her up on her offer, before walking out and disappearing from my sight.

So much for having our little conversation because that had gone nowhere fast.

Sometimes, you had to address issues when they occurred but there were also other times, when you just had to leave shit alone and let it be. It was just that simple. Maybe this was one of those times.

CHAPTER 12

SEANNA

It felt like someone had stabbed me in the chest with a knife and twisted it into my heart as I pulled up at the house and saw Jordan strutting to her car like someone in the Boston Marathon. It was obvious that she was trying to get away before someone spotted her.

Well, it's too late bitch because I see your trifling ass.

The trench coat that she was wearing flopped around as she sped up and I saw that she didn't have many clothes on to speak of underneath as I caught a peek at her bra straps. She unlocked the door and entered her vehicle. She hadn't spotted me as I pulled up to the parking space on the side of the building. I simply sat in my car in awe as she pulled out at the exit directly behind me.

I had been so out of it at work today that Jessie told me to just go home and relax. She had been doing a lot of that lately and for as much as I appreciated her for sympathizing with what I was going through, I realized that I wasn't holding my end of the bargain as far as my responsibilities with Second Chance Academy was concerned. But today, I had decided to take her up on her offer anyhow and it was a good thing that I did because I pulled up, just in time to see what I obviously needed to see.

I was so disappointed in Tremaine and I had no idea what I was supposed to do about it because the man was literally my everything. Again, I felt like I was on the verge of losing control of myself.

After sitting there for twenty more minutes and sobbing uncontrollably, I finally got some perspective and suddenly knew exactly what I needed to do to right some of the wrongs in my life. I was tired of being the victim to people who I was supposed to be able to trust and I wasn't going to allow myself to become anyone else's victim, ever again.

It was time to turn the tide a bit in my favor for once.

After taking a deep breath and colleting myself, I grabbed my purse and fumbled around inside of it until I located what I needed.

My phone.

After unlocking it with my passcode, I searched through my contacts until I found the number that I was looking for. LaKeisha Johnson. A sixteen-year old young woman who I recently came in contact with through her probation agent. She had no stipulations in her probation to join the Academy or anything, but the agent simply wanted me to help her out, if I could, so that she could turn her life around before it was too late. I had developed a positive relationship with the folks down at the probation department and they reached out to me frequently.

I recognized immediately that I would have quite the time convincing LaKeisha to join the Academy. She was a good kid and all, but it just seemed like the streets were in her DNA. But despite her reluctance to join my organization, we had developed quite a little bond and I reached out to her at this time because I had something that I needed her to do for me and I knew that she was all about the money, so this should be right up her alley.

"What's up Seanna?" she asked the instant that she got on the line. "Please spare me on the Second Chance Academy shit today cuz I really ain't in the mood for it."

"What I tell you about that mouth of yours?" I reprimanded in a light-hearted fashion. "That's why your butt always getting in trouble. Did you go to school today, by the way?"

She laughed on her end of the line, finding my motherly posture amusing like always.

"As a matter fact, I did. I'm just getting back in, for your information. But now that I've put in my time at that rachet ass high school, I can focus back on getting this paper."

"How? By selling drugs again or let me guess, by robbing old people at the grocery store like you did the last time that you got in trouble?" There was no limit to the things that LaKeisha was willing to do to get a few dollars in her hands. She was fearless and sometimes, her fearless nature worked against her. But still, that didn't stop her from doing what she felt that she had to do. Depending of what her financial situation was at the time.

"That was then and this, is now," she said simply. "Now, I'm bout to start playing on these thirty ass niggas, since they starting to check for me so hard all a sudden."

"That aint the way LaKeisha," I schooled her but as usual, she wasn't trying to hear any of it.

"I hear you," she said dismissively. "So, if you not calling about Second Chance Academy then why are you calling then because the big sister routine is starting to get a little played out."

"As a matter of fact, I wasn't calling you about anything concerning Second Chance Academy, actually. Although, I definitely think it would benefit you. But you know how I feel about that already, so no need to keep harping on that. Actually, I was calling you because I had other business for you. I guess, you can call it a proposition of sorts."

I now had her undivided attention.

"I'm listening," she said with a business-like tone.

"How would you like the chance to make $50,000 by doing something for me? You won't get paid upfront. But if you do your part effectively, you can expect the money within two to three business days at the latest."

She giggled in excitement.

I measured my words very carefully before continuing.

"I hate to ask something like this of you because I'm supposed to be helping you do something positive with your life. Not come up with different schemes." I paused as I thought about what I was asking of her before deciding that I didn't have any other options right now and pushing forward. "But what can I say, I really need this to happen and I need someone who I can trust because I can't have nobody finding out about this or it will ruin me. Nobody LaKeisha. Only the two of us. So, are you on board or what because I know how bad you be chasing that paper? So, now you got the opportunity to really come up on quite a bit of cash, so long as you do your part without messing it up."

Her end of the line went silent for a second, as she digested everything that I had just said to her.

"Now, you talking my language, boss lady. Like I told you, I'm all about the paper, and you don't gotta worry about me telling nobody shit because I don't fuck with nobody, but myself. That's how I survive."

I knew this to be true because she had been taking care of herself for a very long time now, which was why she was always getting into trouble. Her mother had abandoned her when she was only six years old and she had no idea who her father was. She had grown up in a slew of foster homes but had no real ties to any of the families that she had stayed with, throughout the years. She was now staying with an Indian woman, whom she seriously despised. She didn't listen to anything that the woman said to her and was simply bidding her time till she turned 18.

Her 17th birthday was about two weeks away.

LaKeisha was just looking for an opportunity to get out on her own and getting this type of money would most definitely be a huge step in that regard. So, I was still helping her out at the end of the day.

Even if it wasn't the most ethical or morally-correct thing to be doing with an impressionable, young girl like herself.

"So, now that we have that business behind us and you know where I stand at," LaKeisha said, breaking up my thoughts. "Tell me, boss lady. What exactly is it that you need me to do for you?"

CHAPTER 13

TREMAINE

By the time that Seanna got in, I was just ready to relax and call it a day. OTA's were back under way and my body was tired. The little exchange that I had with Jordan right after getting in from practice, only further served to exhaust me and as I now realized, it wasn't even really worth the effort.

Seanna was a breath of fresh air.

She came in and greeted me in a way that she hadn't in months, which took me a little by surprise.

"Hey bae. How was your day?" I asked, noticing that she seemed to have a lot more energy than she normally did, once she got in from work.

"I'm fine babe. Just ready to be with my man." She took me in her arms and held onto me for a moment. I bent down and gave her a tender kiss.

"You better stop girl before you start something in here," I warned.

"What do you think that I'm tryna do?" she countered with. "You still got some of that white Hennessy left, don't you?"

"I sure do. Why, you wanna try it out finally?" I had been urging her to drink some of it, since one of my teammates brought it back with him for me when he took a cruise to the Caribbean. Seanna hadn't been having any of it. That is, until today. "It's in the bar. You can't miss it. Hell, pour me some to and put just a touch of coke in it for me. You might wanna do the same for yourself, lightweight."

She laughed before proceeding to fix our drinks.

In order to impress her, I downed my drink in record time. She simply watched me in amusement, while slowly sipping hers. I laughed as I saw the tortured expression that was on her face as she swallowed it.

"You don't have to worry about me asking for no more of that stuff. It tastes horrible."

She sat her glass down and grabbed my hand.

"Now, that you're more relaxed, I need you to come back here and do something for me."

I jumped to my feet like a bunny rabbit and followed her to our bedroom so that I could see what she had in mind.

■■

After Seanna and I had sex, I must've gone straight to sleep and evidently, I had been pretty out of it for a while because by the time that I woke back up, it was the next morning. I looked at the clock and saw that it was 7:15. OTA's started at 8:30, so I needed to get a move on.

I had just gotten through taking a piss and was just about to get a pair of boxers out of the drawer, so that I could take a shower, when I noticed that something was sitting on the dresser face down. I picked it up and flipped it over so that I could see what it was, and I almost passed out, right where I stood.

It was a photo.

A provocative photo.

A photo of me and a pretty, young girl, who couldn't have been any older than fifteen or sixteen years old.

I was lying on the bed completely naked beside her and looked to be extremely satisfied and content. She was stripped down to her bra and panties and had her left leg draped over me seductively and was holding my dick with her left hand.

This wasn't a good look at all.

Fear and panic immediately began to consume me.

I checked the house and saw that I was the only one here.

Seanna had probably headed out for work already because she usually went in at about 6:30. But I didn't give a damn about any of that right now because she had obviously been a part of this whole little charade, so I would go down there and confront her in front of everyone, once I got dressed.

By the time that I threw on my clothes, I sat down on the bed and thought about my plan of attack and I couldn't seem to think of anything because I was in quite the fucked-up situation.

My phone rang.

I grabbed it off the wireless charger.

It was Seanna.

I picked it up and began to spaz out immediately.

"What type of shit are you tryna pull off with this picture, huh? You unappreciative, shady ass bitch. Don't play with me! I'll get you touched for real out here, tryna pull some shit off like this!"

She laughed.

"Oh, you think I'm playing with your stupid ass, huh? Try me if you wanna. I'm telling you."

"You ain't gon do shit, but what I tell you to do," she said finally with much confidence. "That is, unless you want that photo to be published, and if anything happens to me, it will still be published, and you will go down for murdering me anyway because you will be the one who had an obvious motive to do it. So, I'm not even worried about that shit right there."

She had obviously done her homework.

I started to say something, but she cut me off before I could even get started. My blood boiled as she began to speak again.

"By the time that I get off work today, you are to have $5,000,000 directly deposited into my account, and don't try to play with me either because I already know that you have my account number and routing number. Don't have it done and I'll show you just how serious that I am."

"Why are you doing this Seanna? This is so unlike you to be scheming like this," I wanted to know as my anger subsided and got replaced by new emotions. Hurt and hopelessness.

She thought it over for a moment before responding.

"I'm doing this because I'm tired of people like you, taking advantage of people like me. That's why."

"But how do you figure that I took advantage of you? All I've ever tried to do was be there for you, in any way that you needed me to. What have I've done so bad to deserve some foul ass shit like this?" I was totally confused and couldn't make sense of any of it.

"Ask your girl Jordan," she said simply, which caused the wheels to start turning.

I couldn't come up with anything.

"I have no idea what you're talking about Seanna. It's not my fault that she went on the air like she did. I had nothing to do with any of it. I don't know why you would believe that I did."

"Who said that you did?" she asked impatiently.

"Then what in the fuck are you talking about then?"

"I saw her leaving the condo yesterday Tremaine. I pulled up just in time to catch her leaving out and I saw what she had on."

I laughed.

"So, that's what this whole thing is about? I didn't do anything with Jordan, if that's what you're thinking. I called her over to have a conversation about the shit that she said on the air and she came onto me then I kicked her out."

She laughed.

"And you expect me to believe some shit like that?"

"Yeah, I do," I told her honestly. "Because it's the truth."

"So why didn't you tell me about your plans to meet up with her then?"

I searched for an answer, but couldn't seem to come up with anything in my own defense.

"Exactly. And why didn't you tell me that she came by and tried to come on to you, since you so damn innocent?"

Again, I was at a complete loss.

"I know it sounds crazy and all but I'm telling you, I did not sleep with that woman, Seanna. You gotta trust me on this. The only woman who I want is you."

She hesitated for a moment, as my words began to get to her a bit. Then, just as I thought that she was about to hang up, she began to speak again.

"I suppose that anything is possible," she said through a voice laced with emotion. "But I'm done taking chances on people, just to continue to be disappointed by them. I'm done taking chances and if you don't want your career to end and become another celebrity turned criminal, you best to do what I told you to do by the time that I get off work today. The choice is yours, Tremaine."

She hung up before I could say another word.

Afterwards, I just sat there, shell-shocked, staring at the phone like it would come to life. I was in a hell of a predicament and there didn't seem to be a damn thing that I could do about it, other than what she asked. For as unfair as it was, I couldn't just allow my reputation to go up Shit's Creek like this. I had worked too damn hard establishing myself to just stand around and allow things to go by the wayside like this.

I called the bank and wired $5,000,000 to Seanna's account.

CHAPTER 14

SEANNA

I was so glad that Tremaine had decided to do the right thing because I would've hated it if I would have had to end the man's career like that, especially after all his hard work. I know that I shouldn't have cared, after the way that he played me and everything, but the reality of the situation was that I did care, and it would've bothered me a great deal if I would have had to do it.

Luckily, it didn't come down to anything so drastic.

LaKeisha was ecstatic once I handed her the money that I owed her. 50 Large. All in big bills. She had done her part. So, now, I had to do mines. She gave me a huge hug and told me that if I needed her for anything, to just hit her up. I told her that I doubted that I would need her for anything in the future. She asked me to keep her number, just in case something came up that she could be of an assistance to me with.

I promised her that I would.

Realizing that I had outstayed my welcome in Kansas City, I decided that I would return home to Columbia. I had plans and I needed to be fully present in order to execute them the way that I intended to.

Boy, were my mama and sisters in for a rude awakening, once I got back home.

Hee hee.

Them hoes had to pay for trying to ruin me the way that they had, and I would see to it that they got, just what they all deserved and more.

But for now, I had one more thing that I needed to tend to before I left Kansas City.

One more acquisition to make.

I had contacted the owner of 107.4 this morning and inquired about buying his radio station. The man's name was, John Lovett. A tall, white man. A little rough around the edges. He seemed to be the type of person who was always in good spirits, no doubt because of all the money that he had at his disposal, and he looked like an extra, straight out of a Clint Eastwood movie.

He told me that he wasn't wiling to sell the syndication outright but for the right price, that he would be willing to sell off a controlling share of the budding radio station's interests. The asking price was $300,000 for a third of the ownership. I agreed to his terms and it became official like a referee with a whistle.

I asked him to give me a tour of my new investment.

He eagerly obliged.

They were just wrapping up the morning show when John led me into the booth.

TK Daniels looked at me with amusement on his face.

Jordan St. Claire looked up at me like she wanted to kill me.

"Hey y'all. Sorry to interrupt like this," John apologized to the two of them, while stepping aside and prodding me to step up beside him.

I happily obliged.

"I would like to introduce y'all to our new co-owner, Ms. Seanna Traylor."

They both stared at me with a dumb-founded expression on their faces. I smiled and winked my eye at Jordan, who was beginning to look like she was about to pass out.

"Anything you would like to say, Seanna?" John asked with a huge smile on his face.

"Well, I would just like to say a few words." I looked Jordan directly in the eye as I spoke, so that she would know, without any doubt in her mind, that my words were mostly intended for her. "First, I would just like to say that I'm glad to now be a part of the family and that I trust y'all to do y'all jobs the way that y'all have been doing them up till this point, knowing that you both still have two-years left on your contracts. So, just continue to do things the way that you've been doing them. But I must warn you both that I'm very particular about the way that this station will be conveyed by our listeners and I will only interfere, if I feel like I have no other choice, but to do so. So, do I make myself clear about that?"

Neither of them said a word, just continued to stare at me like I was an alien, from outer space.

"I said do I make myself clear, Ms. Jordan?" I barked at her, silently daring her to try me right now. Seeing the challenge that was in my eyes, she looked away. Wisely deciding not to test me.

That's a good little girl.

"Yeah, we're crystal clear, Seanna," she whispered with obvious resentment, but I couldn't have given two fucks about what she was going through right now.

To hell with her.

I now owned her career and she knew it.

Fuck up if she wanted to and her ass would be on the unemployment line and I would personally see to it that no other radio station hired her, within a thousand miles of Kansas City.

I would see to that, even if it was the last thing that I did.

"From here on out, you will refer to me as, Ms. Traylor. Seanna is for my friends and colleagues. You are neither. So, don't address me in so informal of a way again. I'm not your homegirl and you will show me the respect that I deserve." John laughed, clearly liking the fire that I had. "And furthermore, John and I have had some discussions with how things will be run around here, now that I'm involved, and you two are to report directly to me. So, do I make myself clear about that?"

They both nodded their heads in the affirmative.

"Any questions?"

This time, they both nodded their heads no, looking like two bobblehead dolls.

"Good." I smiled at Jordan once again. "So, now that we're all on the same page, we can get some things accomplished around here. I will be reaching out to the two of you very soon, so be prepared. Good day now."

Jordan grabbed her headphones, which had been draped around her neck, and threw them clean across the room in obvious anger, shattering them instantly, as John and I left the booth and headed back to the office to discuss more business.

Sometimes, the world that we lived in today could be very cruel and unfair, catching you totally by surprise and hitting you where it hurt the most. But the thing about this world was that you could virtually make your own way in it. Even going so far as to claim it as your own.

So, I decided to do just that at this very moment.

This was my world now.

Jordan   was   just   living   in   it.

BOOK II

ENVIOUS ONES

STILL JEALOUS

PUBLISHER'S NOTE

Visit https://stephenjbrowder.wordpress.com or follow me on Facebook @ Stephen Browder to subscribe to my blog and receive updates on upcoming releases.

P.S

Be a pal and leave a review

PROLOGUE

SEANNA

For as much as I loved Tremaine, I now realized that the only person who was going to look out for me, was me. I had been at the mercy of other people for all my life. Now, it was time for me to start being a little more aggressive, which went against my typical character completely. I had always generally been mild-mannered and soft-spoken. Not the type to speak out of turn, even if I had an opinion that I wanted to share. For that was just how much that I had always been concerned with other people's perceptions of me. But we see just how far that has gotten me in life.

It was time for a change.

Definitely.

I wasn't the vicious type. Probably never would be. But I made a vow to myself that if anybody came at me sideways from this point forward, that I would make them pay the ultimate price for overstepping their boundaries with me and I wouldn't rest, until I did.

Hell, I was already putting things into motion.

Jordan was now at my complete mercy, but I wasn't done with that dirty little thot quite yet. I needed her to feel the misery that she had brought to me, in her own life, and I wouldn't stop until I knew that she felt it completely. But as of now, it was time for me to confront the original sources of my pain, directly.

Hell, it's been time.

Mish and Kina had been against me from as far back as I could remember and they did everything that was humanly possible to make my life a living hell, and they did it, all for what? The fact that our father had been fucking both of our mamas at the same time. Like the shit was my fault or something. Get real. I had something for both of their rachet asses but in order to be effective, I had to get close to them. Closer than they probably wanted me to be right now. I couldn't pull it off from Kansas City, which was part of the reason why I was returning to Columbia.

I won't do anything that will deliberately draw attention to myself. That wasn't my style and I didn't want them to get a chance to defend themselves, against my attack. I wanted to catch them completely unaware. When they were both wide open and vulnerable because hell, that was the way that they had always done me. My moves will be very quiet and subtle and by the time that they realized what was going on, it will be too late for either of them to do anything to stop it from becoming a reality.

They had fucked over the wrong bitch this time, indeed.

My phone started to ring.

I looked at the phone and saw a number that I didn't recognize.

At first, I was content with just letting the call go to the machine but then, I thought about it for a second and answered it before the other party could hang up. I looked away from the phone just in time to see that I was now in Asheville, North Carolina.

About two and a half hours, northwest of Columbia.

I was almost home.

"Hello?" I greeted meekly as I waited for the caller to respond.

"Yes, Ms. Traylor. This is, Vance Palmer, returning your call from earlier. I got your message," he informed me.

I smiled on my end of the line.

"Yes. Mr. Palmer. I didn't recognize your number, so I had no idea who this was."

"Oh, I see. Sorry about that Ms. Traylor. I recently moved to Columbia from Orlando and haven't had a chance to transfer my number over yet."

"Don't worry bout it," I told him dismissively. "Well, I'll lock your number in now so that I can know who's calling. So, do you think that you will be able to do what I need you to do?"

"Why, of course, Ms. Traylor. I see no reason why I couldn't."

We worked out the details and agreed to meet the next day. No use in prolonging anything, longer than I had to.

Plus, I couldn't do anything until I dug up as much information as I could first, which was why I had reached out to Vance in the first place.

He was a private investigator and digging up dirt on people was his business.

When I Googled private investigators in Columbia, his name had been the first one that had popped up on the opening page of the search, so I reached out to him immediately. It didn't hurt that he had excellent ratings from some of the people who had used his services in the past as well.

That was just extra motivation for me.

No need in getting my hands all dirty, when I didn't have to. That was one of the many benefits of having over 4 million dollars at your disposal. I could do what I wanted to do, when I wanted to do it, and it was just that simple for me.

CHAPTER 1

SEANNA

It didn't take me long to get back on track, once I got to Columbia, which wasn't at all surprising, when considering the fact, that this was the place where I had been my entire life. Save the four months that I had been in Kansas City with Tremaine. But things felt a lot different this time around. Mainly, because I was so different. It was almost as if I had been looking at the city through a pair of beer goggles before and had finally sobered up, long enough to be aware of what was going on around me. Kind of like when a man got drunk and smashed a girl who he thought was fine at the club, only to wake up the next morning and behold the Gila Monster lying in the bed, next to him.

But to put it more simply, I finally saw the city for what it truly was.

The thing that I really admired about Columbia was that for the most part, the people that you ran across always appeared to be humble on the surface. Especially, when you compared them to the rude and annoying folks in some of the major cities, like Chicago or New York City, for instance. They weren't nearly as obnoxious as those folks were, although, they also had their ways too. The same person who you saw going to the opera and rubbing elbows with the city's elite, you'd catch out in the woods in camouflage, hunting wild hogs, by nightfall. It was amazing. Almost as if they lived a double life, like a special agent for the government Secret Ops division. But the thing that I loved about Columbia the most was that it always appeared to be growing and expanding.

It was a place where a young woman with hunger and more importantly, assets could go and really begin to establish herself.

I stayed in a hotel for my first week in town, but it wasn't long before I found myself an apartment. After looking at about two places, I absolutely fell in love with an upstairs unit in a new development on Greystone Boulevard, around the corner from the zoo and oncology center.

I went to Whit-Ash Furnishings and found everything that I needed to make my new apartment feel like home. Tremaine had gotten me an all-white Dodge Challenger when I had first gotten to Kansas City, so that I would be able to get around comfortably. It had matching interior and a pair of 28-inch Diablo's with white inserts in the middle. *Damn, I missed that man already. Oh well. He was the one who had fucked up, not me.* Even though we had fallen out, I had been fortunate enough to have the vehicle in my name and before I had left Kansas City, I made it a point to also get the title in hand. So, after cancelling his insurance and picking up my own policy, I was all set as far as a vehicle was concerned and I was more than ready to get my new life underway.

Toast, to new beginnings.

After formally meeting Vance Palmer and getting the rundown on the information that he had been able to gather up until this point, I had enough to go off to begin to put my plans into motion. All that I had to do now was bid my time and find myself something nice to wear for tonight, and when I say nice, I'm not talking about looking cute for your mama at church kind of nice or stunting at the mall with your homegirls kind of nice. I mean, shut every other bitch down in a 50-mile radius of me kind of nice and hoe, don't even try it kind of nice.

For the look that I was going for, I jumped on I-26 and headed to Harbison. I wasn't in the mood to trek all up and through the city, just to try to throw an outfit together, so I decided to just go to Columbiana Mall and call it a day.

After going to Macy's and Hollister, only to come up disappointed, it wasn't until I hit New York & Company that I found what I was looking for. The moment that I walked into the store, my eyes became fixated on a light blue, illusion, lace sheath dress that was hanging on the display. It was from a designer that I had never heard of named, Adrian Papell, and it fit over my contours flawlessly. I couldn't dish out the $360.00 for the dress quick enough, which I thought was a hell of a bargain for a dress of this magnitude.

Once I left out the store, I ran into Macy's and grabbed the pair of lace-up heels that I had been eyeballing earlier. They were white with light blue heels that blended them in with the dress perfectly.

Now, I was ready to do some serious damage.

I smiled as I thought about the possibilities.

By the time that I went to the apartment and got myself together, it was showtime. I was a little nervous because I had always been a little reserved. Not the confidant, aggressive woman that I needed to be tonight.

Girl, you got this, I reminded myself before grabbing my keys and heading out the door and to my destination.

∎∎

It was 10:30 by the time that I arrived at, Red's Nightspot.

The age limit for Red's was 21 and up and I was only 20, so I wasn't sure if I would be able to get into the club or not, but I was intent on trying anyhow. This was the exact reason why I had gone for a more mature look tonight because I wanted to blend in effortlessly. By the time that I strutted through the parking lot and approached the entrance, my heart was pounding in my chest like a bongo, but I tried my best to keep my cool.

"Hey sexy. I must say, you wearing the hell outta that dress ma'am. I know yo man must be the happiest nigga on the planet," the bouncer said, looking like a broke down version of, Terry Cruz.

"For your information, I don't have a man," I flirted while reaching out and stroking his right arm, which he had on full display with the sleeveless shirt that he was wearing. "If I did, I surely wouldn't be in a place like this, mingling with other men."

He smiled, staring at me like I was a piece of candy.

"True indeed. You should let me take you out sometime, I'd show you a real nice time. I can promise you that," he offered with much insinuation in his tone.

"I don't know," I told him while appearing to give it some thought. "Let me go in here and get a couple drinks in me right quick. I need to get my mind right. It's been a long, stressful week. But I'll be back out here to kick it with you later. I'll see what you're all about then."

He grinned like the joker as he opened the door for me, so that I could enter the establishment. I had that fool so wide open by giving him the illusion that he might get some pussy tonight, if he played his cards right, that not only did he forget to ask to see my ID, but he hadn't even made me pay the ten dollars for admission.

Now, that I had that business behind me and had finessed my way inside the club, I could focus on the real business at hand. I had someone real important who I needed to accidently bump into tonight.

His name was, Malik Redman.

He was the owner of the club, which was probably the reason that it was called Red's. But that had nothing to do with the reason why I was so interested in him.

I could care less about any of that.

I needed a man in my life who would absolutely adore me and walk to the ends of the Earth for me, so long as I gave him what he needed to keep him satisfied. Malik was a very good-looking man with his chinky-eyes, long, neatly kept dreads, and chiseled body. He reminded me a little of the rapper, Future, and I was very attracted to him, so I seriously doubted if keeping him satisfied would even be an issue for me to begin with. But I didn't know if it was just his good looks alone that attracted me about him so much, or if another element was also coming into play. Maybe there was something hidden beneath the surface that I couldn't see but could somehow, sense, or maybe, just maybe, it also had a little something to do with the fact that he was with my trifling ass sister, Kina.

CHAPTER 2

MALIK

When I first got into this club owner thing, I was so optimistic about where it would take me. You couldn't tell me that I wouldn't be sitting on a fortune by now. If you tried, I probably would've laughed in your face because I thought that I had it all figured out. I was just about as green as they came. Although, I didn't realize it at the time. But now, 4 years have passed, and I was no better off than I was when I first started and that was unbelievably humbling. I thought that I would be sitting on high, by this point, instead of barely generating enough money to keep the doors open.

But that was my reality.

I was starting to feel like I may have gotten in over my head and I had no idea about what my next move would be, but I realized that I had to figure out something.

Of course, no one knew what I was going through. My homeboys and certainly, not my girl. Everybody thought that I had it all figured out because I kept my fronts up so well. But the truth was that I had debt up the ying yang. I had promoters in my pocket. I had investors in my pocket. The bank. The list went on and on. But nobody needed to know what I was going through, but me, because I was the only one who was responsible for making sure that everything ended well.

Kina was the last person in the world who I would tell about what I was going through.

I wasn't no damn fool.

She was so proud of the fact that I had my own business, that she boasted about it, every chance that she got. She brought it up to anyone, who cared to listen, even though I had told her on more than one occasion, to pump her brakes on broadcasting our good fortune because there were people out here who preyed on that kind of thing. She still, continued, to do it anyway, throwing our success in the faces of some of our friends and associates, who she perceived as being less fortunate than us. I just hoped that it didn't all come crashing down on us because they would all, no doubt, rub our noses in it because of her obnoxious ways.

That wouldn't be a good look at all, but we would've brought it completely upon ourselves. So really, we had no one else to blame for it, but us.

Now, don't get me wrong. Kina wasn't a bad person at all. Just a little selfish and shallow. But if she fucked with you like that, she had a heart of pure gold. There was no denying that. She was just so damn preoccupied with the way that people looked at her that it was sickening.

It really was.

In the year that we had been talking, she always appeared to be jockeying for status. She almost appeared to be obsessed with it and I just couldn't seem to figure out why. I knew nothing about her upbringing, other than the fact that she had one sibling. An older sister named, Misha. Whenever I tried to dig any deeper into her family life, she deflected the conversation to something else, as if she wasn't in the mood to elaborate on it much. I always left it alone, figuring that she would get more in depth when she was ready to do so.

I had never really been much of the pushy type, but I was really starting to wonder about what all she had been through in life to make her the way that she was.

To be completely honest about it, there were times when I felt that Kina was only with me because she felt that I complimented the image that she wanted to portray so well that she did virtually anything that I asked her to do for me, without any ifs, ands, or buts about it. I loved her for this but also realized that she did it, only because she thought that I was the man and wanted to keep me in her life, which made me wonder what she would do if I ever fell off and had to get a regular job to make ends meet. Just like most other people did.

I had a feeling that it wouldn't be pretty at all.

Should I even stick around long enough to find out? Was what I found myself debating about a lot as of late.

I would try to figure all that out at another time though.

As of now, I had a business to run and the night looked to be a bit promising, so I needed to be present in the moment. It was a Friday night and we had a decent turnout. Had to make sure that everybody had a decent time so that they would continue to come back and see me and tell a few friends about my club.

After briefly mingling with a few of my regulars, I introduced myself to some of the new faces who had come out to the club tonight. Mostly women, as they were usually the ones who were the most receptive to me. The fellas normally went where they went, so there wasn't no need in wasting my time trying to make a good impression on them. One lady, amongst a group of five, made a pass at me. She was dark-skinned and shapely. She actually reminded me a lot of my lady Kina, but she wasn't half as pretty. I flirted back but kept it vague. The way that I was accustomed to doing with my customers. She said that it was her birthday. I told her that I would get her and her friends a round of drinks, compliments of the house.

I headed to the bar so that I could place their orders with one of my bartenders when I looked to my left and saw her.

A light-brown vision of perfection.

Off to the far end of the bar, sat a beautiful woman in a silky, baby blue dress and she appeared to be alone, for as hard as that was for me to believe, just looking at her. She had full-shoulder-length hair that bounced with every movement that she made, and she had pretty-pouty lips that would've put, Meagan Good's to shame. What I liked the most about her though was that she didn't have on hardly any make-up to speak of and had some of the most gorgeous skin that I had ever seen in my life. She had just enough curves to do the dress that she was wearing serious justice and I could see that, even as she sat in her chair.

Even though, the place was crowded, she somehow managed to stand out, amongst everyone else who was in attendance tonight and for some reason, I just couldn't seem to keep my eyes off her.

No matter how hard that I tried to.

Not wanting to get myself into any trouble, I said a few more words to my bartender, Tameka, before turning away and making my way through the club. I looked to the far end of the bar once again and was surprised and a little disappointed to see that the woman was gone. Deciding to make my own departure, I headed to the DJ booth and told the DJ that I would take care of him in the morning. Having previously done business, he said that he had no problem with that at all. I turned around just in time to bump into the woman from the bar, and when I say bump into her, I meant that literally.

She fell to the floor as I tumbled over her.

I reached out and grabbed a nearby chair, which was the only thing that kept me from falling on top of her.

Sheesh.

"I'm so sorry sweetheart. I guess, I wasn't paying attention where I was walking," I apologized with a horrified expression on my face while reaching down and helping her to her feet, catching a glimpse of her laced Victoria Secret panties in the process.

Damn, this chick was sexy as fuck and I had run her over like a goddamn fool.

Seeing what I saw, two male onlookers tried to beat me to the punch, but I told them that I had it under control. They stared at me for a minute, as if I was cock-blocking or something, before reluctantly backing off.

"It's okay," she said while grabbing her elbow in obvious pain. "I know that you didn't do it intentionally or anything, so it's cool."

"Naw, that's not cool," I insisted. "I could've seriously hurt you, walking into you like that. Thank God that it wasn't worse. I feel like I owe you something. Go have a few drinks on the house. My treat."

She shook her head, as if to say that none of that would be necessary.

"Thanks for the offer and everything, but I'm not much of a drinker. Besides, I was just about to head out, so you don't even gotta worry about it."

"All right now. I just don't want you to go home and tell your man that the owner of Red's tackled you down to the ground and have him come up here and whoop my ass or nothing."

She laughed from the picture that I had painted.

"Well, you don't even gotta worry about that because I don't got a man to tell. So, if anything, I would be the one to come up here and beat your ass myself," she said jokingly with a teasing smile on her face, which made her look even more gorgeous than she was already. If that was even possible.

"Is that so?" I wanted to know while staring at her like she was a piece of meat.

"Yessir," she said simply.

"But you gotta let me do something for you. I insist."

She took a second to give it some thought.

"Okay. Since you wanna do something for me so bad, I was leaving here so that I go grab a bite to eat. I would tell you that you could treat me as a means of paying me back, since you insist and all. But there is one little problem though."

"Such as?" I asked with feigned impatience.

She laughed again, picking up on all of that.

"I already ordered a pizza and it's too late to cancel the order. By the time that I get home, they should be pulling up."

Disappointment instantly washed over me, as the thought of this beautiful specimen in front of me, walking out of my life forever, never to be seen or heard from again, began to hit me like a ton of bricks.

"I could always come there to pay for it," I offered, only half-jokingly, knowing that she would probably never go for that in a million years.

I looked up and was surprised to see her actually considering it.

"I don't know about you coming to my house and everything. I don't know about that," she debated to herself. "It would be okay, I guess. Only if you promise to be a gentleman and behave yourself, once you get there." She looked at me for confirmation.

My heart did a somersault in my chest.

Something about her tone told me that she didn't want me to necessarily behave myself, once I got there, but we would see.

Yes, we would most definitely see about that.

What a wonderful night this had turned out to be already and the best part about it all was that it just kept getting better and better.

"Scouts honor," I said while holding up a peace sign like I had saw the, Cub Scouts, do on TV, when I was little.

"Cool," she said while turning away towards the east parking lot. "I'm parked over there. Walk me to my car, please?"

I did as she asked.

Once we got to her vehicle, she unlocked the doors and told me to get in so that she could drive me to mines. I was parked in front of the building. She took me to my car. I hopped in and proceeded to follow her to her house.

I had no idea about what was about to happen, nor was I overtly concerned with trying to figure it out. All I knew was that with this woman, at this time, was exactly where I wanted to be. I had never been any surer about anything in my life. So, I would just go with the flow and hope that when it was all said and done then, if nothing else, that I would've at least had a memorable experience because if things kept going the way that they were going with my business then the day would, eventually, come when I might not have nothing left, but my memories.

CHAPTER 3

SEANNA

Luring Malik to my apartment had proved to be much easier than I anticipated that it would be. I had been a little unsure of myself with me never have done anything like this before. But the more that I actually went out and did it, the more confident that I found myself becoming and I liked it.

I liked it a lot.

As promised, the pizza man pulled up a few minutes after we got there. Malik settled the tab and I escorted him upstairs to my apartment. He complimented my place and took a seat on the couch. I asked him if he wanted any. He said that he was straight. I threw a few pieces on a paper plate and sat down on the couch next to him.

"I know you not about to sit there and demolish all that with as little as you are?" he inquired with an amused smirk on his face.

"You don't believe me, just watch," I told him before turning back to my plate and proceeding to do just what I promised him that I would.

He watched in amazement.

"You are not playing over there," he said while I finished off the last slice.

I got up to fix myself something to drink. I felt him looking at my body as I turned my back on him and headed to the kitchenette.

I smiled and put a little extra sway in my hips, for his benefit.

"Have any," I offered once again.

Again, he said that he was straight.

He asked me what I did for a living. I told him that I did a few odds and ends to make ends meet and left it at that, not wanting to say too much or too little. He asked me was I from Columbia. I told him that I was and asked him the same. He told me that he was from Sumpter but had been in the Met since he was about ten years old. He was thirty, so he had been here long enough to know everything about the way that the city functioned.

We talked a little more, about nothing in particularly, before I decided to cut it short.

"For as much as I'm enjoying our conversation and all, I have to admit that I'm starting to get a bit tired. It's been a long day, so I think I'mma take it in the back and shut it down."

His eyes instantly flashed with disappointment.

"I understand darling. To tell you the truth, I'm starting to get a little tired myself, so I'll get out your hair."

I stared at him in confusion.

"What's the matter?' he asked, noticing the way that I was looking at him all a sudden.

"Nothing, I suppose," I whispered. "I guess, I thought that you would come in the back and join me. Maybe I'm being too forward."

"No, no," he stopped me immediately by grabbing my hand before I could walk away. I turned back towards him and looked up and met his gaze. He bent down and kissed me softly on the lips.

"Oh my," I said afterwards as I struggled to catch my breath.

I looked at him again but this time, no one said anything. He followed me closely as I led him down the hall to my bedroom.

I told him to take a seat on the ottoman at the foot of my bed as I slowly began to disrobe.

He stared at me in awe as I exposed myself and he couldn't take his clothes off quick enough. I beheld his manhood for the first time, and I wasn't overtly impressed by what he had to offer, but I put on a performance that would've made Halle Berry do a standing ovation as I carried on about how big his dick was and how I didn't want him to hurt me with it because I had never been with a man who was as large as he was.

He promised me that he would take it as easy on me as possible.

I said nothing in response.

Just continued to stare at his dick with a concerned expression on my face like I was dealing with Mandingo, himself.

I'll admit that it felt funny having another man on top of me, besides Tremaine, but after much effort on my part, I slowly adapted to it. It took a while but eventually, I found his rhythm. I wouldn't exactly say that we were in synch with each other as I rocked my hips back and forth and he thrusted his into me like a jack rabbit, but by the time that Malik exploded into the condom and stumbled to the bathroom to clean himself up, I realized that I had him exactly where I wanted him.

CHAPTER 4

TREMAINE

Once the season kicked off, I was back to my usual routine and suddenly, nothing else mattered to me but reaching the promised land. I always locked back in, during this time of year, because we had a lot of rookies and recently signed free agent acquisitions who I wanted to set a standard for. I was one of the leaders on the team and took my responsibilities seriously, knowing that we wouldn't get anywhere this season without strong leadership in place.

Besides, I was on a contract year and needed to show the league how much of a complete player that I had become, since entering the league three years ago. That way, I would have more available options when I became an unrestricted free agent next off season. For as much as I preferred to stay in Kansas City and finish my career in the place that had taken a chance on me, when others wouldn't. At the end of the day, this was a business and I would most definitely move on to greener pastures, if the price was right.

I had just gotten out of practice and was leaving the facility when I was approached by a familiar face in the parking lot.

It was Jordan and I had half a mind to walk right pass her, after everything that she had put me through with Seanna. But once I studied her closer and noticed the stressed look that she had on her face, I decided to hear her out, despite myself.

"Tre. I'm not tryna come down here and bother you or nothing. I just needed to talk to you about that girl of yours. She tripping for real."

I started to tell her that Seanna and I were no longer together but decided against it, when I realized who I was talking to.

She would probably use that shit against me, somehow. Was the conclusion that I quickly came to as I put it aside in my mind.

"Why? What happened?" I asked with great interest as I pushed the remote start so that the engine could heat up, even though it wasn't very cold out.

Old habits die hard.

"You know that chick done went in partnership with the owner of the radio station where I work at, don't you?" she asked, just for the sake of doing so, assuming that I already had this knowledge.

I decided to play it off and act like I did.

"Okay," I said impatiently. "And you say all that to say what exactly?"

"Well, I guess she done decided to cut back on a few things, and it was all good when it involved some of the more frivolous things, like free lunch from restaurants and free tickets to shows and whatnot, but now she fucking with my salary and that shit ain't cool at all."

She was obviously quite upset, but I seriously doubted if Seanna cared anything about how she felt about this situation, or else, she probably would've never done it in the first place. It was hard to get someone to sympathize with you when you were the one who instigated the action to begin with.

That was like asking the Jews to be lenient on Adolph Hitler had he suddenly, been thrown in the concentration camps with them, during the Holocaust.

Some things simply weren't going to happen, no matter how badly that we wanted them to.

"Well Jordan, that is rather unfortunate and everything, but what do you want me to tell you?" I had no answers for her and felt no need in pretending like I did, so I decided to go ahead and put that out there to her so that she wouldn't be mistaken about it. "I have absolutely nothing to do with the things that are going on down at your radio station. As you mentioned, Seanna is in business with y'all, not me. So whatever beef that y'all may have with one another, y'all will have to work out, amongst each other, and it's pretty much that simple. Sorry I couldn't be more of an assistance to you."

She sucked her teeth in irritation. I shrugged my shoulders and told her sorry, once again.

"Well, when you see her again, you need to try to talk some sense into her. I'm just tryna warn you, Tremaine. I'd hate to really start dragging your girl out here because she won't be able to recover from it this time, trust me. And you know I can do it too, don't you?"

I said nothing.

Mostly because it wasn't my place to say anything.

Now, don't get me wrong, I knew Jordan, and I knew more than anyone else just how calculated and ruthless that she could be when she wanted to be. But in these last few months, I have saw something different in Seanna that made me feel like she could go toe-to-toe with anyone who came against her.

It was scary to even imagine my sweet little Seanna ever becoming this type of individual, but here we were. I knew that I had something to do with this unpleasant transformation in her because it was me who had introduced her to this life in the first place. Therefore, I had to take some responsibility for it. Even though she had straight fucked me over by leaving me the way that she had behind some pure bullshit, there was no way that she could've known that, so I fully understood why she had done it.

I didn't like it, but I understood.

Even though, I was pissed at first, especially by the way that she wasn't even willing to hear me out at the time. Now, that I've had a moment to examine everything from every possible angle, I really wasn't even all that mad about it anymore.

If I wanted her back, I had to go out there and get her back like a man.

It wouldn't be easy.

She might not even want to hear shit that I had to say about it.

But I had to make her listen to me anyway.

If I wanted things to be back right between us, it was up to me and me alone, to find a way to make it right again, so that I could get my lady back in my life before she strayed too far from within my grasp.

CHAPTER 5

SEANNA

After that night at the club, Malik called me every day for a week and left me countless voicemails. Some pleading, some borderline-threatening. Just as it appeared that he was about to reach his breaking point, I called him up and invited him over so that we could have a little chat, which he promptly agreed to.

It was time to take this thing to the next level.

The instant that he walked in the door, I was on his case about the secret girlfriend that I found out he had. Of course, he naturally denied it at first. Just like the typical man would under such circumstances. Questioning me on where I got the information from so that he could know who to watch out for. But I wasn't having any of that.

I told him in no uncertain terms, that he was to let her go and never deal with her again or he could forget about me and him ever dealing again. He agreed to my terms and told me that he would do whatever it took to make me happy. I told him to prove it. He asked me how. I told him to call her right now, in front of me, and break up with her so that I could hear him do it.

"Don't you think that's a little cruel?" Malik asked in amazement, not believing that I could expect him to carry out such a request.

I stared at him without an ounce of remorse in my eyes.

"You have a choice Malik. It's either gonna be her or it's gonna be me. I can't make you do a damn thing you don't wanna do." I shook my head, as if I couldn't believe that I was actually having to have this conversation with him right now. "And to think that I was actually thinking about helping you expand your business. No sir. Not for this shit."

The mention of his business got his undivided attention.

"Excuse me? Come again?"

"You heard me right Malik. You probably don't know this about me, but I'm an investor and I've recently been looking for some businesses in the area that I can help expand and become profitable, so because of the line of business that I'm into, I talk to the folks down at the bank a lot. I was going through a few portfolios when guess whose little nightclub came across my radar?"

He dropped his eyes down towards his lap as he realized where exactly I was going with all of this.

"I was surprised to see that you had been so financially irresponsible," I scolded as if he were my child. "I see you're into the bank for about 50 Grand and have an undisclosed lien out there on top of that. So, I figured that hey, I like this guy. I like him a lot actually, and I have some money to throw into his business, but why in the world would I be willing to do that when he wasn't even my man?"

With that, he looked me directly in the eye.

I smiled.

"And who says that I'm not your man?" he asked with a serious expression on his face, not willing to allow this opportunity to pass him by.

"Just the fact that I asked you to do something to prove your devotion to me and you haven't done it yet, tells me everything that I need to know about you sir."

I watched in silence as he removed his phone from his pocket and dialed Kina's number. He put it on speaker so that I could hear the whole exchange.

"Hey bae. You just left and you missing me already?" she said the instant that she got on the line, sounding about as bubbly as I'd ever remembered her being.

This silly bitch was about to be in for a rude awakening.

"Hey Kina. I ain't call to do a lot of talking," Malik explained while staring directly into my eyes, so that I would know that he meant business. "This shit between us just aint working out no more for me."

Her end of the line went silent for a second, as she tried to make sense of what he had just said to her.

"I hate that it has to be this way, but it's over. Time for us to move our separate ways."

"But why Malik?" she groveled between hoarse sobs. "What did I do to deserve this? I try to do everything that you ask of me."

"It's not that. It's just that I feel that it's time to move in a different direction. That's all. Ain't nothing you did," Malik explained with a remorseful tone that I didn't care to hear in his voice.

I shot him a look of disapproval.

"Don't do this Malik," Kina continued to beg. "I'll do anything to make things right between us again, if you just give me another chance. Why are you doing this to me, Malik? Why?"

"Because he done met a bitch better than you and who has her shit together much more than you do, that's why," I piped in with, causing her end of the line to go silent for a moment. Malik stared at me in anger. But I couldn't have cared less about what he was going through right now.

Never have, to be completely honest about it.

"Who is this hoe?" Kina asked in anger, once it registered that her man was breaking up with her in the presence of another woman. "I'll fuck yo' ass up."

"I'm your worse nightmare bitch. The motherfucka that you love to hate. Now, you got a reason to hate me hoe."

"I know that voice. When I figure out who you are, I'm gonna come whoop yo' ass. I can promise you that," Kina threatened, even though I knew that she wasn't about to bust a grape in a fruit fight.

"You and Mish couldn't do it before back at Roberta's. What make you think you can see me now? Get real." I laughed on my end of the line, as if she was absolutely hilarious to me because she was.

"Seanna?" Kina asked in disbelief, sounding like she was talking to a ghost.

"In the flesh," I told her without a bit of hesitation. "The two of y'all used to love to hate on me for no reason at all, when all I needed was for y'all to show me genuine love and support, so now, I guess, you actually got a real reason to bitch and I'm perfectly fine with that."

I hung up the phone before she could say another word.

She tried to call back twice.

I sent her to the machine both times.

Dumb bitch.

Some people just didn't know how to take no for an answer.

Malik looked at me like he wanted to slap me, once he realized that the two of us already knew one another, and that he had been getting used by me the entire time. I told him to relax and eased his mind by removing a slip of paper from my pocket and handing it over to him.

He stared at me in amazement as he read the receipt that absolved all his debt from the bank. I was now the lien holder of his club and I had every intention of clearing it completely. But that was conditional, of course.

It was up to him really.

Do what I asked him, and he would be able to start from scratch, debt free, in no time. But if he chose to try me in any shape, fashion, or form, I had no problem turning his little club into a recycling yard.

CHAPTER 6

MALIK

I can't believe that I had allowed this chick to play me like this. Kina probably would never speak to me again and I couldn't blame her, if she didn't. It was obvious that she was hurt. She had never made it a secret the way that she felt about me and for as skeptical as I had always been about it, due to her shallow ways, now that I had ended the relationship and I saw the way that she had reacted to it, I was starting to think that maybe, there was some genuine love there, after all.

But for as much as I still cared for her, there was just something about this chick Seanna that I was feeling more. She brought more to the table and that was the type of woman who I needed to build with.

Not somebody who I had to do everything for like Kina.

Once the air cleared, my curiosity caused me to ask Seanna how her and Kina knew each other. She said that they were half-sisters and that Kina and Mish used to dog her out, on a daily basis, when she was forced to live with them when she was sixteen. Simply because their mother didn't like her mother. I told her that I had never heard Kina make mention about having a sister, besides Mish. She laughed and said that she didn't at all find that hard to believe because they both hated her guts. It was sad and now I understood why she had reacted to her the way that she had on the phone. Well, she had obviously come out on top now, so I guess the joke was on the two of them, when all was said and done.

Before I could ask any more questions, she told me that she needed me to do something important for her. I asked her what it was and told her that I would do anything that she needed me to do. She smiled at me warmly and told me that I was too sweet.

"I need you to call Kina and tell her that you wanna get back together and that you stopped dealing with me, once you found out what I was all about. Then, I want you to invite her and Mish down to the comedy house tomorrow night. I have three tickets for y'all for the ten o'clock show." I went to the back and grabbed the tickets that I had purchased yesterday off the nightstand and handed them over to Malik.

"Then what?" he wanted to know with a little unsurety in his voice. "What's the move after that?"

"You let me worry about that baby. I just need you to do what I asked you to do."

"You're not gonna do anything crazy, are you? Cause I'm not tryna be a part of no shit like that."

She shrugged her shoulders, as if it didn't make a difference to her one way or another.

"Suit yourself. But I was prepared to clear you of this lien, after you made this happen for me. But if you can't help me, then I can't help you. It's just that simple."

She was playing me like a puppet, and I knew it. But at the same time, I had to do what I had to do.

"All right. You got it. I will do what you asked but I promise you that I'm not getting in the middle of any more of your personal shit with your sisters, so are we clear on that?" I was dead serious. She looked me in my eyes and wisely decided not to challenge me about this, seeing that I was no longer willing to compromise.

"Crystal clear," she said through an innocent smile that I wanted to slap clean off her face.

"So, do you want me to call her now or what?" I asked, just ready to get this whole little charade over with so that she could give me what was promised to me.

"No. That won't be necessary. You can call on your time. Just make sure that they both be down there at about a quarter to ten because I don't want them to miss the show." She laughed as she said that, which caused an eerie feeling to wash over me.

Now, what in the hell did this fool ass girl have planned exactly?

I didn't even wanna know.

Sometimes, the less that you knew about something, the better off that you were.

CHAPTER 7

SEANNA

It took me about twenty minutes to get to the Comedy House on Decker Boulevard, due to an accident on Park Lane. I knew that I should've came straight down Two Notch Road but noooo, I had second-guessed myself. Like I sometimes liked to do.

I told Malik to text me once they arrived. He told me that the three of them would be riding together. Little did he know that I had invited somebody else to the show tonight. Alexis' older brother, Antonio.

From as far back as I could remember, Antonio had been in and out of prison, mostly for petty offenses that he served less than a year for. He was a pretty cool guy. Just couldn't get out of his own way. No one would hire him because of his lengthy track record and most of the things that he did, he did only because he needed to make some ends meet.

I had told him to be down at the Comedy House at 9:30 and he was there, as expected. He had his instructions, so he was only bidding his time. 15 minutes later, they arrived. Malik texted me once he turned into the parking lot as he was instructed to do. I texted him back and told him to park on the side of the building.

He did as he was instructed.

I smiled, realizing that this was the moment that I had been waiting for.

The instant that they stepped out of the car, Antonio approached them. To be such a tough-looking woman, resembling a slimmer version of Cleo from, *Set It Off,* Mish appeared to be awfully shook as Antonio closed in on them. I stepped out of the car and approached them as well.

"I just brought him here for back-up. In case you two bitches got outta pocket," I informed them once they got within earshot.

Mish stared at me like she wanted to kill me as I walked up on them. Malik had a look of unsurety on his face as well, not knowing what to expect. Kina stared at me with fire in her eyes but said nothing because she already knew what it was.

"So, what you want hoe? You brought us down here, so start speaking," Mish demanded as if she was calling the shots. I nodded my head to Antonio. He swung on her instantly, catching her squarely on the chin. Dropping her down to the ground instantly. Shocked, Kina tried to run to her sister's aide, but I swung on her before she could get very far.

"You stupid bitch. You ain't never gonna be shit!" she cursed me while wiping the blood away from her busted lip. Malik just stood by helplessly, not knowing what to do.

Before she could say another word, I ran up on her and hit her again and again.

"You just gon stand there and let them do this to us?" Kina asked Malik before I caught her with a clean one that sent her spiraling to the ground. Antonio now had Mish pinned down to the ground, against the curb. She struggled to break loose but didn't get very far. He was too much for her to deal with.

"Now, I want y'all dirty bitches to listen to me and listen to me good. We are not children anymore and I'm not putting up with y'all dragging my name any longer. Do the shit again and you won't have to worry about doing it ever again. Try me if you think I'm bullshitting."

"Fuck you," Mish belted out through a mouth full of blood. Kina panted angrily. I watched her closely and grinned once I realized that she didn't have any more fight in her.

Weak ass bitch.

I ran up and kicked Mish in the face from where she laid. She immediately lost consciousness.

I handed Malik the lien certificate, which I had already signed over to his name. Kina stared at him like he was a traitor and refused to let him touch her as he tried to help her to her feet. Mish was just starting to come back to when Antonio and I walked away. I paid Antonio the $5000 dollars that I had promised him to carry out this task for me and jumped in my vehicle and headed on my merry way.

I would no longer have to worry about either of them, I realized, and that was the way that I preferred things. For so long, I have been a victim to people who I was supposed to be able to trust, just to get stabbed in the back time and time again by them, whenever I let my guard down around them. I wasn't going for that shit no more and I would use whatever means that I had to in order to make sure that they were showing me the proper amount of respect.

CHAPTER 8

TREMAINE

Once Seanna and I parted ways, I didn't even want to entertain the possibility of dealing with another woman for a while, and that was exactly how I kept it for the better part of two months. Focusing instead on football and conditioning, and things that would just make me a better all-around athlete. It wasn't until my strength coach put me on a program at the local fitness center, that I wavered from my plan.

There was a woman down there who I took an immediate liking to, but only from a physical sense.

Her name was, Felicity Carmichael, and she was bi-racial. Pretty enough in the face with a body that would've made Serena Williams start hating on her. She was a dance instructor, mostly Zumba and mixed aerobics, and the man in me wanted to see just how talented that she was with that sick ass body of hers. As it turned out, she was a huge Kansas City fan, so getting her to come to my place that evening wasn't much of a hassle.

She had just finished a class and still had on her dance clothes, once she arrived. But she did have a change of clothes with her in a duffel bag and asked if she could take a shower and get herself together. I told her that she could. No sooner as we were in the back and I was getting her a towel and a rag out of the linen closet, I was all over her. Kissing her neck, grabbing her titties, squeezing her ass, which was surprisingly soft for a woman who was so fit.

She moaned and threw her head back, so that I could continue kissing on her neck.

"Tremaine, it has been so long since I've been with anyone that I just can't seem to control myself. I didn't know that I would respond like this," she lied while reaching down into my shorts and stroking my dick as it began to awaken.

I proceeded to help her out her clothes. Not in the mood for much conversation. I needed some pussy and I needed it bad.

We would save all the chit chat for later.

For now, the only thing that I wanted to hear was our skin slapping together.

Her body was even more gorgeous naked as it had been at the gym in the tight clothing that she had been wearing. This girl was ripped, without an ounce of body fat in sight. My dick began to throb in anticipation.

She dropped down to her knees and yanked my shorts down to the floor and began to gobble me up like Ms. Pacman. I grunted as she increased the speed. She knew what she was doing. There was no denying that. Not wanting to cum before I saw what that pussy was like, I made her stop and guided her to the bed.

She tried to lay on her back in a missionary position, but I had other plans. Instead, I grabbed two pillows from near the headboard and propped them under her knees as I put her on all fours. She was only 5 '2, so she needed a little elevation so that I could have a better driving angle. I opened the bedside drawer and reached in and grabbed a magnum out of the pack. She rubbed her clit as I ribbed it open and slid it on.

"Fuck!" she shouted as I slide all 9 inches of me inside of her for the first time. Her inner vaginal walls pulsated with every stroke that I took.

I felt like she had a little hand in her pussy, holding me in. For that was just how tight that she was.

Maybe she hadn't been lying when she said that it had been a while since she had been with anyone.

Once I really got to bearing down on her, she tried to get away from me, but I grabbed her around the hip with my right hand and spread her ass cheeks apart with my left so that I could plunge even deeper into her canal.

"Goddamnit Tre. . . Hold up. . .Wait a min. Uhn! Please, wait. Uhn! I think I'm bout to cum!"

I continued to punish her with reckless abandon as I felt my own moment on the horizon.

She squirted all over me, which was a first.

Still, I didn't let it stop my momentum. I proceeded to pound into her even harder.

She tried to get away from me by crawling towards the head of the bed. I crawled with her and pinned her down once she got trapped by the headboard. She squealed like a wounded animal as I continued to take her roughly from behind and this went on for about ten more minutes, until I finally came and put her out of her misery.

She playfully punched me in the arm afterwards.

"Nigga, you tryna kill me or something?" she asked, playfully outraged.

"Naw darling. I just got caught up in the moment, I guess. C' mon so we can go clean ourselves up."

She followed me to the bathroom so that we could both jump in the shower.

Even though, I was physically satisfied, for the time being at least. Emotionally, I felt terrible and didn't plan on repeating this act, any time soon. Now, don't get me wrong, there was nothing at all wrong with Felicity. Under any other circumstances, I would definitely ride this thing out because that was some of the best sex that I had ever had in my life. So, it most definitely wasn't that. It was just that I wasn't happy having meaningless sex with random women. I had done that before and it wasn't for me.

I had never been that guy.

When I spent my time and energy on a woman, I liked to think that it was actually going somewhere. That's not to say that things couldn't evolve into something deeper with Felicity or anything. I had no doubt that it could. But the problem was that I didn't even want to find out if it would because my heart still belonged to another woman.

Seanna had been on my mind like crazy lately and I knew that I had to do something about it. The crazy thing was that not even a week would pass before I had my opportunity to get her back in my life, once again.

I guess it was true that everything in life happened for a reason.

CHAPTER 9

SEANNA

I had been so preoccupied with my sisters and Malik that I almost forgot that today was the big day. If it wasn't for Alexis calling me and reminding me about my appointment today, it would've been all the way over with. Thank God that I had asked her to join me last week. Everything happened for a reason, indeed.

After getting myself together and grabbing a quick bite to eat, Alexis had arrived. I ran to her car like a gust of wind and we jumped on I-20 and headed to Broad River Road.

There were some very important people who were expecting me today, and I wouldn't have missed it for the world, or my bad memory. Whichever one ended up vanishing first, between them.

A feeling of doom immediately washed over me once we got to the women's correctional facility where my mother was being housed. Apparently, she had went back to court on appeal and had been able to get her original sentence reduced to a lesser offense, which was why she was up for parole now, after only five years.

The parole board allowed one close family member to appear before them at parole hearings on behalf of the prisoner and since I was the closest family that my mother had, they issued me a formal invite to the event.

I was probably the only family member that they had on file, was the conclusion that I came to. My mother had been an only child and had lost both of her parents, before I was even born. I had never known any of my cousins.

The only other family that I knew, besides Mama and Daddy, was Mish and Kina and we see just how great that all turned out.

I accepted the invite without a bit of hesitation.

After getting cavity searched and allowed entrance into the facility, we were led down a long, barren corridor. Alexis was told that she would have to wait in the lobby because I was the only one permitted to attend the hearing. She was already aware of this, so it came as no great surprise. One of the CO's who were escorting us, veered off with her and led her to her destination.

"Right this way ma'am," his burly, white counterpart instructed as we continued to trudge along down the corridor until we got to a set of double-doors at the end of the hall. I felt like I was walking my last mile and couldn't even imagine being in such a place for any length of time. I couldn't see how Mama did it. But, I guess, she didn't have much of a choice in the matter.

He opened the doors and stepped aside so that I could enter the room. I looked around and took in my surroundings.

Three older white men sat behind a podium, who were serving as the council, and Mama sat at a solitary desk facing them, cuffed and shackled like a crazy woman. An armed CO stood directly behind her. I'm guessing that he was the peacekeeper in case Mama became hostile, after they reached their decision. It was crazy because I had never saw the woman even so much as get into a physical altercation with anyone in my entire life, and now they needed a trained officer who was no doubt, a sharpshooter, to keep her under control?

Talk about a reality check for your ass.

Mama's hair was braided in cornrows, which was a style that I had never seen her rock before when she was free. My mama had always been the dainty type and had never cared for anything that didn't express her femininity. So, this new and improved Ole G Bobby Johnson style that she was rocking now was a culture shock, and she was fully attired in prison blues, making her look like a true inmate. It broke my heart to see her like this, and it hurt, even more, when she looked at me and smiled.

I didn't return the gesture.

Just simply stared at her with a neutral expression on my face.

Underneath her rough appearance, I still saw the same woman who used to sing Angela Winbush songs to me at night, until I went to sleep. It was because of her that I went crazy every time that, *I'll Be Good,* came on the oldies station. I still saw the same woman who used to brush my hair at night and made me look in the mirror and tell her what I liked about myself, and she wouldn't let me look away until I did it either.

She later told me that she used to do this because she wanted me to know my own self-worth and she felt that the best way to accomplish this was by getting me to fall in love with myself. Over, and over again. It was an interesting concept and maybe this had aided in the positive self-image that I had of myself, but if this was true, the other reason would have to be the undeniable fact that I knew that I looked so much like her.

She was beautiful to me.

So, I felt that if I looked so much like her then that meant that I had to be pretty damn all right, myself. Even if I was a little darker than she was, and my cheekbones didn't sit nearly as high up on my face as hers did. I loved her. Always had. So, I couldn't help but to be affected by all this.

But despite what I had going on internally, I snapped back to reality and reminded myself that I was here because I had a duty to fulfill. No one said that this was going to be easy, but it was my job to perform, so I had to own it.

I wasn't allowed to speak at this hearing, even though I had been allowed to attend it. But that was fine. I didn't need to speak anyway. I had already gotten the words across that I needed to when I handed my letter to the commissioner. He read it then addressed the committee.

"It seems like we have an interesting development. Seanna Traylor, Mrs. Buckner's daughter, gave me this letter to consider before we make a decision on her mother's fate and I think that we really need to consider it," The Commissioner informed the other committee members. They nodded their heads in agreement and then proceeded to read the letter that I had just given him.

To whom it may concern,

My name is Seanna Traylor and I am the daughter of one of your inmates, Mia Buckner. I realize that my mother is eligible for parole today and for as much as I would love to see everything work out in her favor, I have to be honest with everyone down here because that's my duty as a Christian.

With that, Mama's head snapped in my direction.

I pretended not to notice.

From as far back as I can remember, my mother has always relied on everyone to do everything for us, but herself. For the longest, we had my father around to provide for us financially, even though I later found out, that he also had another family to support, which my mother was fully aware of, mind you. It wasn't until he left us for good that my mother resorted to stealing people's identities to survive. She even tried to pull me into it, asking me to steal household bills from some of my friend's parents, so that she would have their information, when I went to their homes to hang out with them, and I'm ashamed to admit that I did it for her. It was wrong, even if I was just 13 years old. I knew it was wrong, even then, and I did it anyway. But understand that I only wanted to help my mother out, in any way that I could. I realize that this doesn't justify anything, but that was my reason for doing it.

The committee members stared at her like she was a monster for asking something like this of her child.

It was bad enough that she had even been doing it in the first place, but to get your child involved like that was just straight sick in their eyes. The Commissioner stared at her in disapproval before looking back down at the letter and reading from it again.

I only wanted to help her out, he picked back up with. *So even though I would like to see her regain her freedom again one day, I ask that she receives some type of counseling first and learns some type of trade that will help put her in a better position, once she returns to society because for as much as I love her and I really do, I just don't want her living the way that she did before. I want her to be the woman that I know that she's capable of being.*

"Thank you for that, Ms. Traylor," the commissioner said with a sympathetic smile on his distinguished face. "I know that sometimes, the hardest thing to do is to come down here and be honest about your loved ones. Most people don't realize that you're only hurting them when you lie to protect them. So, just know that you did the right thing young lady, by coming down here today and being honest with us. We could use more people like you in the world, and I mean that."

I smiled in appreciation before looking back down towards my hands.

Mama glared at me like she wanted to kill me.

Maybe it was a good thing that she had on the cuffs and shackles, and the trained killer was nearby.

I know it made me feel a hell of a lot safer, knowing that he was there. But I'm just saying, though.

Together, we watched in silence as they headed to the back to convene. Ten minutes later, they reemerged as they came to their decision.

By the time that they finished speaking, you could hear a pin drop on the floor. For that was just how deathly quiet that it was all a sudden when it was announced that Mama's parole was denied.

She would see the board again in 2024, on the date that she had been scheduled to see them, originally, before getting back on appeal.

"Why Seanna? Why did you do this to me?" She shouted out at the top of her lungs as the CO forcefully escorted her out of the room.

I said nothing.

Really, nothing needed to be said.

Now, she knew how it felt when the one person in the world who you depended on the most, straight shitted on you like you were nothing. She wasn't bitching and moaning about it when she had given Jordan all that false information about me for a couple of dollars on her books, so don't bitch about it now.

Besides, she had more important things to worry about right now, like making sure that she fulfilled all the things that were required of her by 2024, so that she wouldn't be in this same position the next time that she went before the committee and making sure that she didn't drop the soap in the shower tonight.

CHAPTER 10

MALIK

This whole thing with Seanna had gone too damn far now. The spell that she had cast on me had officially worn off and I was livid, particularly after the way that she had done Kina and Mish, in the parking lot, of the Comedy House. But surely, she had to have a reason to be so vengeful. People didn't just get that damn mad for no reason. Plus, even in the heat of the moment, I remembered Seanna mentioning some things that led me to believe that she had been mistreated by both Kina and Mish and was just simply reciprocating the punishment that she, herself, had received from their hands.

I asked Kina about it and she instantly got defensive, but I knew her well enough to know when she was hiding something, and she most definitely was. So, realizing that I wasn't about to get anywhere with her, I decided to turn to her sister instead.

Mish had always been more of the straight shooter between them and in the year that we have been talking, the two of us have built a little rapport. I wouldn't exactly say that we were cool like brother and sister because that would be a definite stretch. But we had a mutual respect for one another and were comfortable enough around each other, due to our familiarity, that it wasn't weird when we spoke on personal things.

I called her up and asked her if I could come through.

She told me that she didn't have a problem with that, so I jumped in the whip and headed her way.

The guy that Seanna had gotten to attack Mish, had done quite a number on her. Both of her lips were busted, and she had the beginnings of what look to be forming into a nasty shiner on her right eye. She looked like she needed to be in somebody's hospital. Not sitting on the couch, shooting the shit with me.

I told her that she looked terrible and that I felt weak as hell for not jumping in and getting that nigga off her then promptly went to explaining my reasons for standing pat, before she could get upset about it. She twisted her face, but said nothing, as she processed everything that I had just told her.

"So, what's going on with her and Tremaine?" she asked as another thought came to her. "They not together, no mo'?"

This was the first that I heard mention of this name.

"Tremaine? Who the hell is Tremaine?" I asked, completely lost.

Mish looked at me like I was the biggest idiot in the world.

"Tremaine Simeon. You know Tremaine. Dude play running back for Kansas City. Him and Seanna are engaged. Or, at least, they were the last that I heard about it."

My jaw dropped to the floor as I realized that I had been banging out the fiancé of one of my favorite running backs in the league.

"You can't be serious, right now?" was all that I could manage under the circumstances.

Seeing the look that was now on my face and reading my thoughts like a fortune-teller, Mish said, "I bet you really feeling yourself now, aint you pops?"

"Hell naw. He just a nigga like me. His money just set up a l'il different than mines, that's all. I ain't never been the groupie type. That shit don't mean a damn thing to me," I lied as I tried to keep my ego in check.

"I heard that," Mish said, not buying a word of it.

It was time for me to get to what I came to find out.

"So, tell me Mish, and I want you to be completely honest with me about this, but what did y'all do to Seanna for her to come at y'all the way that she did at the Comedy House?"

She studied me closely, as if trying to figure out how much that she wanted to tell me about their family issues. I stared back at her in a way that told her that I wouldn't back down until I find out what I had come to find out. After a brief stare down, she looked away in defeat.

"When Seanna came to live with us, after her mama went to jail, let's just say that we probably weren't as sensitive as we should have been towards her," Mish admitted, sounding a little regretful while looking me directly in the eye. "Our mama had never liked her mama and I guess, we had taken it out on her, which was really silly, I now realize. She is our sister and she was dealing with a lot back then. Probably still is, and instead of being there for her, like we should have been, we did everything to make her life a living hell. Even after she got herself in a position to do better for herself. We still gave her hell."

So, Seanna was their sister. Kina had never mentioned that part. But she wouldn't, would she.

"And here, I was, ready to ride down on her for attacking y'all when in reality, y'all had brought this whole thing down on yourselves. Unbelievable." That was why I never liked to get involved in anyone's family shit, right there. You could never get the truth from both sides, so you were always shooting blindly.

"I never asked you to do that," Mish told me through a serious expression on her face. "The only thing that I need you to do is tell me where that bitch lives at and don't try to lie either because I know that you know, Malik."

Suddenly stuck between a rock and a hard place, I tried to talk some sense into her before this thing escalated any further.

"But what you need to know that for? You just said yourself that y'all usedta dog her out, right? Surely, at some point, you knew that she would try to get back at y'all," I reasoned.

Mish shook her head, as if she wasn't trying to hear any of it.

"True. I knew that eventually she would get sick of the shit and come back at us, but she should've kept it verbal, like we did. Having a nigga come jump on me like that was beyond crossing the line and that bitch definitely has to pay for this shit."

I couldn't help but to feel where she was coming from but still, I didn't want to have any further involvement in this thing, and I told her as much.

But once again, she wasn't trying to hear any of it.

"You got involved when you started riding with that bitch, over Kina, behind that miserable ass club of yours, and I'm trying really hard right now not to send those dogs knocking at your door too. It would be in your best interest right now if you just told me what I needed to know. Trust me on that, my dude."

I had half a mind to just raise up out of there and be on my merry way, but I knew Mish well enough to know that she very rarely gave empty threats. Plus, I had saw firsthand, some of the dudes who she was affiliated with and I really didn't need that shit in my life, right now. I had my club back and was no longer in any debt to anyone, anymore. Things were definitely looking up for me and I clearly didn't need to be out here, trying to prove how much of a man that I was to no damn thirsty ass clowns. That lifestyle was a thing of the past for me and I didn't plan on regressing, anytime soon.

Mish smiled as I grabbed the pen off her coffee table and jotted down Seanna's address. She told me that she appreciated me for it, and that I was safe, at least for the time being anyway. I said nothing as I made my exit. There was no point in following her up. They could beat the brakes off Seanna.

It didn't mean a damn thing to me.

CHAPTER 11

SEANNA

Now, that I've put my mama in her place and showed her that you couldn't just do whatever you wanted to do to people, without having to face the consequences, I was content with just moving on with my life. You would think that she would've known that already, especially with her being in the place that she was in for attempting to get over on someone before. But still, she had managed to fuck me over, even from in there, which was why I didn't feel bad at all about what I had done to her with the parole board.

What was good for the goose was good for the gander, I had always been told.

Now that this business was behind me, I needed to figure out my next move. I had conquered everyone who had stood up against me, so I didn't have anything left to prove, anymore. It was time for me to start laying down some roots somewhere.

It was during these moments that I began to think of Tremaine and the life that we could've shared together, if his dick hadn't gotten in the way. I'll admit that I still kept track of him, even though it has been eight months since we've been together. I guess, I hadn't gotten over him completely yet.

Probably never would.

I realized that he had more than likely moved on from me, by this point, and had probably found another love interest to occupy his mind. But still, thoughts of him consumed me and I knew that I would never be able to move on to the next phase of my life until I reached out to him and got a bit of closure. I went back and forth with myself for a while until I figured what the hell and gave him a call. A part of me hoped that he wouldn't pick up the phone so that I wouldn't have to face him. But in true Tremaine fashion, he answered on the first ring, effectively eliminating that possibility.

"Hello?" he greeted, obviously not recognizing the number. I had gotten another phone since I left Kansas City, although I had kept my contacts, and I now had a local number.

"Yeah Tremaine, it's me. Seanna," I told him through a shaky voice, not really knowing what to say, besides that.

Suddenly, his end of the line went silent. For a minute, I thought that he had hung up on me, but then he spoke, and I knew that he was still there.

"Hey Seanna, how you been doing?" his voice had suddenly softened, which caused my heart to pitter patter in my chest a little.

"I've been good Tremaine. How about yourself?"

"Well, I'm as about as good as can be expected, considering the fact I no longer have you in my life."

Now, why did he have to go off and say something like that?

I became infuriated.

"Well, you were the one who messed that up, Tremaine. Not me. I mean, what in the hell did you expect me to do, just sit around and allow you to do me dirty like that?" This man was incredible. But, yet, for some reason, I was the one who felt guilty about it.

He was just that damn convincing.

"I told you already Seanna, I did not sleep with that woman."

So, he was still sticking with the same story, after all this time, even though I had basically caught him in the act.

"If you don't believe me, ask Jordan about it," he said.

I had never even considered that possibility. Just to see if there was any validity to his claim. I needed to talk to her anyway about some things that were related to the show, and that would give me the perfect opportunity to check her temperature on this issue. But I wouldn't tell Tremaine about all that. I didn't want to give him an opportunity to prep her before we spoke.

"Well, that's neither here nor there," I told him dismissively. "So, what's been going on with you? I know that you're probably seeing someone by now? A good-looking man like yourself."

"As a matter of fact, I'm not. But I know that you probably are, by now. I'm not stupid. I figured that much." There was so much disappointment in his voice as he said that last part that I couldn't help but to smile a little on my end of the line.

It wasn't that I wanted him to be miserable or anything because he didn't deserve that, whether he had done me wrong or not. It was just a little flattering to know that he still cared about me enough to actually get jealous over someone who he assumed that I was dating.

"No Tremaine, I'm not seeing anyone. After going through everything that we've been through, I just needed to take a break on the relationship thing for a while. Take care of some loose ends in my own life. You know what I mean?"

He agreed that he did, before getting back on the subject of him, and, I, getting back together.

I shook my head, thinking that this man was impossible to deal with.

"Actually Tremaine, I won't bullshit you, I have been thinking about you a whole lot lately. No matter how hard I force myself to try not to. But I just don't know if us getting back together is the right move or not. Hell, for all I know, you could still be bitter with me about the whole money thing and want to make me pay for it, once I got back around you."

Tremaine laughed at that.

"Is that what you've been thinking all this time? Hell Seanna, I would have given you 5 million dollars, had you simply asked for it. Hell, I still would, even though we're not together anymore. I love you that much baby. Money doesn't mean shit to me when it comes to what's in my heart, and you are the woman who still has my heart. I don't want nobody else to have it, but you. In my eyes, you will always belong to just me."

That was enough to make me emotional because I knew him well enough to know that he meant everything that he was saying right now. I collected myself before I spoke again because I didn't want him to know that he was having this affect on me.

Had to stay strong.

"And how are things going with Second Chance Academy?" I asked, changing the subject.

Before I left Kansas City, I had turned the organization over to Tremaine, even though it had been my thing. The way that I saw it, I was no longer going to be in Kansas City so I wouldn't be much of a benefit to it anyway. Plus, after blackmailing Tremaine out of 5 million dollars, the way that I had, I figured that turning the organization over to him was the least that I could do. Even though it was a non-profit, I figured that he could still recoup some of his loss by writing it off, during tax season.

"Oh, Second Chance is still doing fine. Waiting for you to come back home and take it to the next level."

This man was relentless, and I had always loved that about him.

I didn't even want to talk about him and me until I spoke to Jordan and got some clarity. But as I mentioned before, I didn't want him to know my plans, so I dismissed him by promising him that I would give him a call tomorrow and agreeing to have a much more, in depth, conversation about things that pertained to the two of us then. Hearing that I was starting to waver to his charms, he let me go, without putting up much of a fuss about it.

He was too smooth to squander his opportunity by being impatient with me.

I took a minute to regroup before scrolling through my contacts until I ran across Jordan's number. I wasn't sure if I was doing the right thing, but I knew that I had to do it, so I dialed her number before I completely lost my nerve.

She picked up with an attitude.

"Yes, Ms. Traylor? Can I help you with something?" Unlike Tremaine who hadn't had my new number stored in his phone because I had never called him from it, since I left Kansas City, Jordan did because I reached out to her a lot more often with me being the co-owner of the radio station that she worked at. I mostly called her to check her on something that she had said on the air that I didn't care for, and the shit drove her crazy too when I did it, which was probably the reason why I kept on doing it.

"Listen Jordan, I know we haven't always seen eye-to-eye and I realize that I'm just as much to blame for that, as you are. So, I'm willing to do better under one condition," I offered without any hesitation, deciding to get straight to the chase.

"And what's that?" she wanted to know with much interest in her tone, clearly tired of having to deal with my shit, whenever I reached out to her.

"I want to know what happened between you and Tremaine, the day that you came to our apartment."

Her end of the line got silent.

"Did you hear me?" I asked, not liking the way that she had ignored the question. I was just about to ask her again when suddenly, she began to speak. I held my tongue so that I could hear her out.

"Yeah, I heard you. Why do you need to know what me and your so-called fiancé discussed?"

The insinuation in her tone told me that she was aware that Tremaine and I were no longer together. For as much as I tried to disguise it.

"Let's just say that I have my reasons," I told her simply, knowing that I still held the upper hand as far as she was concerned.

"I can tell you," she began with. "But why would I wanna do that? Basically, what I'm getting at is, what's in this for me, because I'm not the type to kiss and tell?"

She was fucking with me, and I knew it. But still, I needed her right now so I would play this little game with her until I got the information that I needed.

"If you tell me what I want to know then I will start laying off you down at the radio station and let you do your thing for now on, without any interruption from me."

She gave it some thought.

"Naw. That ain't good enough for me darling. I will tell you everything that happened, only if you agree to leave the radio station completely," she offered in an uncompromising tone.

Little did she know that I was thinking about selling my share of the radio station anyway because truthfully, I had no use of it anymore. The only reason why I had even purchased it in the first place was to fuck with her for doing me the way that she had with Tremaine. But I was starting to evolve, so I no longer had any interest in the petty shit.

I agreed to her terms.

She wanted guarantees.

I told her that I wasn't about to put anything in writing, if that was what she was looking for, but that she had my word on it, so she would simply have to trust me on it. She told me that she didn't trust anybody when it came to business. I told her that it was up to her and attempted to end the conversation when she stopped me short.

"Okay, I'll take your word on it," she barked out abruptly before I could hang up. "But I'm telling you Seanna, if you play me, I will come after you with everything that I got and believe me, I know some folks who can make some shit happen. I'm telling you. Don't even try it."

Even though, I wasn't really worried about her little threat because it didn't move me whatsoever, she didn't have to worry about me reneging on my word because I planned on following through with it. I had bigger things planned for myself and realized that I wouldn't be able to sustain anything that I tried to build unless I first, eliminated all the bullshit that I had going on in my life.

Like I said already, I had evolved pass the petty shit.

It didn't have anything to do with her.

"Like I told you before, I'll keep it clean, so long as you tell me what I wanna know," I told her for the second time. "I'll keep my end of the bargain. I wouldn't have reached out to you if I was on some bullshit. I'm not you. I don't do shit like that. You know, smile up in people's faces, acting like we cool and shit, just to stab them in the back later when they got comfortable around you. You know how you do. So, you good, baby. You can trust what I told you. You ain't even gotta worry about that at all." I couldn't leave it alone without taking one final parting shot at her because she was really a despicable individual.

"Good," she said impatiently, clearly feeling like she had gotten her point across to me.

I let her think that she had.

"Now, that we have that understanding, we can talk like two grown women are supposed to," she continued with. "Ask me whatever you wanna know, and it don't have to just be about Tremaine, either. It can be about your mama, your sisters, I don't care. I'll tell you anything that you wanna know."

With that, her end of the line went silent as she waited for me to respond.

I collected myself then leaned back in the chair and began to ask my questions.

CHAPTER 12

TREMAINE

It took everything that I had in me not to call Seanna that next day but as to not come off as being thirsty, I forced myself to fall back until she called me. Day turned into night and night turned into the next day and still, I hadn't heard back from her yet.

Had she given me the flag salute and was no longer interested in me? I began to worry. But if she had, there wasn't a damn thing that I could do about it anyway, I realized. For as hard of a reality as that was to accept.

Hounding her about it wouldn't accomplish a damn thing, so I mine's well fall back and focus on the things that I could control.

We had just played our final preseason game against Arizona and had two weeks left before the regular season kicked off. Coach had given us the day off and wanted us to gear our minds towards the long, grueling season ahead. My mind was always geared, so that wasn't much of a problem for me.

I chose to spend my time studying tape instead.

We opened the season at home, against Miami, who had made the playoffs last year. They were a mediocre team at best but did have a formidable defense that we had to diagnose, and it didn't help that they were returning a lot of their starters from last year. I watched for an hour before I started to pick up on some of their tendencies. I wrote a few things down that I would share with Pat, our Offensive Coordinator, in the morning. I was wrapping up my media session when my phone began to ring. I snatched it off the couch, where it had been lying, face down, and looked at the screen.

It was Seanna, finally calling me back like she had promised to do.

Giddiness washed over me, but it proved to be short-lived once I answered the phone and actually heard her voice.

Something was wrong, and I recognized that immediately.

"Hey Seanna, is everything okay darling? I was wondering when I would hear back from you," I fired off immediately, not the one to mince words.

She took her time about responding.

"I just wanted to tell you that I owe you an apology," she said finally. "I talked to Jordan yesterday and she basically corroborated everything that you told me happened, between y'all two, and I know she's telling the truth, so I feel like such a goddamn fool right about now."

"It's okay," I coaxed her, wanting to capitalize off the momentum that I now had working in my favor. "I would've had a hard time believing that stuff myself, so I definitely understand what you were going through, trust me."

"No, it's not okay. It's not okay at all," she insisted. "I should've believed in you, just off the strength that you had never given me a reason not to. Just goes to show how mentally fucked up that I am, I know."

"You are not fucked up mentally," I told her, not liking the way that she was belittling herself, which was so unlike her.

"Yes, I am, Tremaine. You just never realized it, that's all. But I just wanted to call you and apologize for falsely accusing you the way that I had. Well, that, and I also wanted to thank you for being so good to me when we were together. No man has ever made me feel the way that you have, so thank you for that."

Why did it feel like we were saying goodbye to each other?

I didn't like the sounds of this at all.

"No need to thank me, Seanna. I was just doing what a man is supposed to do. What 'your' man is supposed to do. Hell, in my eyes, I never stopped being your man, even though you tried to push me out your life," I sounded desperate right now, but I couldn't have cared less because that was just how much that I loved Seanna and needed her back in my life.

"I wish things could go back to the way that they were before," she whispered with a dream-like quality to her voice, as if she was replaying all the things that we had been through together, over again, in her mind, as we spoke.

"And who says that they can't go back that way? Who says that they can't be even better, the next time around?" I demanded to know as my frustrations began to set in. I felt like I was losing her, and I didn't know what to do to stop it from coming into fruition.

"I wish they could, Tremaine," she admitted. "But now, it's too late. Too much has happened, since that time, to turn back now and pretend like it's all good because it isn't, and that's just the way that it is."

"Tell me Seanna, what happened so bad that the two of us can't figure it out together? Tell me that please because this shit just don't make no kind of sense to me." I wished that I could reach out and touch her right now and tell her that everything would be all right, but we were almost 1000 miles away from each other so the only thing that I could do was express myself to her verbally and hope that my message still somehow, got across to her.

"Let's just say that I'm not the same girl who I used to be, Tremaine, and I'm not so sure that I even want to be that girl anymore, to be completely honest with you about it."

Again, that dismissive feeling began to flood me.

"And who says that I want you to be the same girl, Seanna? I love the woman that you've matured into being and I accept you, however you come. You should know that by now."

Now, why in the hell had I said that?

"What the fuck you mean, however I come? It kind of sounds like you're implying that I was nothing before the two of us got together. Is that what you think of me, Tremaine?" she drilled me with the instant that the words escaped from my mouth.

"Now, I never said nothing like that Seanna. Those were your words, not mines."

It was a weak ass response and I recognized that immediately.

"Well, you don't have to say the words, Tremaine. You implied it and that's enough for me. Or did you think that I was too dumb or wasn't cultured enough to pick up on that type of thing?"

I tried to explain myself, but she cut me off before I could get a single word out of my mouth.

"And here, I was, feeling all bad and shit for not wanting to be with you anymore, after everything that I felt that you had done for me. But now, I realize that you had never really did anything for me. All the stuff you did was strictly for your damn self. So long as I waited on you hand and foot, it was all good. But the minute that I try to actually find myself, it's a problem for you."

She was more upset than I could ever remember her being, save the time that she thought that I was creeping with Jordan.

"So, you're gonna sit here and act like I've never done anything for you, Seanna? Really? You gotta be kidding me with this shit." Now, I was beginning to get a little upset because what she wasn't about to do was completely discredit everything that I had done for her like it was nothing major.

I had done more for her financially than I have for all the other women who've I dated before her, combined, so that wasn't anything to take lightly.

"So, what have you done for me exactly, Tremaine? I wanna hear this, so please enlighten me?" Her tone was patronizing, but I tried my best to ignore it as I spoke.

"What I've done for you," I repeated through an incredulous tone. "How about get you everything that you needed when you didn't have a dime, or sponsor your little non-profit organization just because it was something that you were so passionate about? Not to mention just give you five million dollars when I could have just as easily had said fuck it and disputed you in court. The list goes on and on Seanna, so don't even try to play me like that."

She laughed.

"Typical," she said with subsiding laughter.

There wasn't a damn thing funny about this to me.

"What you mean by typical?" I asked feeling like I had really put my foot in my mouth this time by saying too much.

"Just the fact that you've had been keeping score about the things that you've done for me, proves that you had been doing it for yourself the entire time. Just so you could throw it back in my face, like you are now, whenever it benefited you to do so. That's not love Tremaine. That's being possessive and controlling. But you don't have to worry about none of that no more because the days of me being your little project are over and done with, so please, take good care of yourself, sir."

She hung up the phone before I could get a chance to explain myself.

The hope that I had of the two of us getting back together now appeared to be a lost cause.

Something had gone terribly wrong here and at the end of the day, I had no one to blame for it but my damn self, for speaking so out of turn. For as much as it bothered me to do so, I just had to man up and live with her decision and hope that once the sun set over the horizon and one season turned into the next that somehow, Seanna would find her way back to me. If not, that would be the true definition of what a tragedy was.

CHAPTER 13

SEANNA

Talking to Tremaine took all the energy that I had left in me and the only thing that I wanted to do was be by myself and try to figure everything out. It had been very hard for me to come to this decision, but after thinking long and hard about it, I decided that going backwards wasn't going to get me very far in life. So, for as much as it pained me to do so, I knew that I had to let him go, once and for all.

Whether he had cheated on me or not.

I was no longer the same Seanna that I had been when we were together, and I didn't feel that we were all that compatible any more. Tremaine wanted a woman who was willing to be his sidekick and didn't mind living in his shadow, content with all the extravagant things that he did for her without asking any questions about it. I wanted to make my own way and didn't want to be in anyone's shadow any longer, so really, I had no other choice but to severe ties between us and find my own way.

Nobody said that it was going to be easy but sometimes, you just had to do what you had to do and put the emotional shit on the shelf.

Even though, I didn't owe her anything, I had decided to keep my word to Jordan. She had done virtually everything that I had asked of her, so it was only right that I kept my end of the bargain in exchange. Didn't want any bad karma by reneging on my word at the last minute.

I didn't need that shit right now.

So, despite my better judgement, I called John Lovett and told him that I wanted to sell him back my shares of 107.4. He asked me why I wanted to do this all a sudden, and I informed him that I had other things that I needed to focus my attention on right now and could no longer show the type of dedication that I preferred to be able to, as far as the radio station was concerned. He told me that he understood where I was coming from completely and let it be that.

John asked me what would be in this deal for him, if he was to even consider it as a real possibility? He was a shrewd business man, which was the reason why he was as successful as he was as a capital investor.

You didn't reach the level that he was on by mistake.

He didn't do anything unless it benefitted him in some way.

After giving it some thought, I told him that I was willing to part with my 1/3rd share of the syndication for only 75% of my original investment, which was absolutely bananas from a business standpoint, when taking into account the fact that the business was on an upward trajectory and had been steadily for the last three quarters. He promptly agreed to my terms, realizing that he would be making a $75,000 profit while also retaining exclusive ownership of the radio station's interests.

We agreed to put it in writing on Monday.

His lawyer would contact my lawyer by then to work out all the tedious details that were involved in a deal like this.

So, now that I had all this business behind me, it was time for me to clamp down and figure out my next move. Whether it consisted of leaving the country and starting over some place else or simply finding a new direction to head in, right here in the States, I didn't know. The only thing that I was sure of right now was that I wouldn't budge until I figured it all out, and I didn't care if it took all night or all week for me to do so either. I would lock myself in this apartment, completely secluded from the rest of society, until I found a sense of purpose, and I meant that from the very depths of my soul.

I was watching a movie on Lifetime about a woman who had been switched at birth, who had just met her biological parents for the first time. It was an intense movie, especially when you considered yourself actually being in that situation like I liked to do when I watched these types of movies. I was just really starting to get into it when I was suddenly interrupted by the doorbell. Not expecting any company today, I pressed the monitor and asked who it was with a bit of an attitude.

Malik's voice came over the intercom.

I know this crazy ass dude didn't just pop up at my damn house? I thought to myself as a new stage of anger began to manifest itself. It was time to set his ass straight so that he wouldn't make this same mistake again. After a brief hesitation, I buzzed him in. Once he got up to my third-floor apartment and knocked on the door, I snatched it open, prepared to tear him a new one.

But as it turned out, I wouldn't even get an opportunity to.

Before I could get a word out of my mouth edgewise, Malik barged into my apartment with Mish and Kina, in toe. I tried to keep them out by planting my foot behind me and pushing the door back towards them, but they had been able to overpower me, without much of a hassle on their part.

Kina had a gun pointed directly at my head as she entered the apartment behind Malik. She instructed me to take a seat on the couch and shut the fuck up or promised to blow my brains out, where I stood. I stared at her defiantly, prepared to give her all the hell that I had within me, even if it cost me my life as a result. Seeing that they weren't getting anywhere, Mish decided to speed up the process.

She reached back and hit me with everything that she had in her. I tried to fight back but didn't get very far. Before I could gain any type of an advantage, Kina joined the party and the next thing that I knew, she was pinning my arms down to the floor while Mish continued to assault me with powerful, defenseless blows.

Malik walked out the apartment and slammed the door shut behind himself, obviously content with letting the two women handle their business, no matter what it wound up costing me in the end.

I didn't remember much after that.

It had happened so quickly that I hadn't been able to process it fully.

Apparently, I had lost consciousness somewhere throughout the whole exchange because by the time that I came back to, Mish and Kina were gone.

Everything on my body hurt as I tried to regroup and get to my feet. I was exhausted and hardly had the energy to move myself, but I knew that I couldn't just lay here like a dead body.

All that I had to do was get to my phone and I would be able to call someone to come out here and assist me because it was painfully obvious that I wouldn't be able to do this alone.

A sharp pain shot through my leg and I hollered out in agony as I attempted to put weight on it for the first time, since being attacked. I tumbled back to the floor and bumped my head as I landed awkwardly. I collected myself as best as I could under the circumstances before reluctantly reaching down and grabbing my right leg. It was throbbing by this point and something was obviously very wrong with it.

I hollered out again once it registered that the leg was broken, directly beneath the knee. I would later find out that I had a broken fibula from what appeared to be sharp blow. The medical staff told me that I had probably been stomped by my assailant repeatedly in the region, when I lost consciousness. But for as tough of a pill as this was to swallow, it wouldn't be the only horrendous news that I would receive in the wake of this devastation.

The devastation that came at the hands of two women who were supposed to love me, unconditionally.

CONCLUSION

SEANNA

By the time that the police and ambulance arrived, I discovered that not only did Mish and Kina nearly kill me, but they had also ransacked my apartment and found my banking information as well, which was probably the main thing that they had come for in the first place. They managed to extract nearly 2 million dollars from my savings account before the bank blocked them, due to suspicious activity. Wiping out over half of the liquid assets that I had, in my name.

One of the detectives asked me if I had any idea about who may have done this to me because it was pretty obvious that I had allowed the assailants entry into the apartment, due to the fact that there were no signs of forced entry. I thought it over for a minute before telling them that I had no clue about who it could be. They didn't buy the story for one second but couldn't exactly force me into telling them anything, so after hassling me a little longer about it and continuing to get nowhere with it, they decided that I was on my own and left it alone.

I could've just as easily have taken Mish and Kina down, but I was tired of going back and forth with them.

Let them have the money.

If that was enough to keep them satisfied and out of my life for good, then so the hell be it. I still had more than enough money to live off, so it wasn't exactly like they had left me hurting for anything. Maybe they would actually do something positive with it, now that they had it at their disposal, so that they wouldn't end up being bitter at the world and the people in it, like their mama, Roberta, was.

I had stooped down to their level and attacked them first. It wasn't like I was exactly innocent in this whole thing, so there was no point in sitting here and pretending like I was. Only a fool would believe that they wouldn't have tried to retaliate, after the way that we had done them at the Comedy House. I had brought it upon myself, so now, that was all behind me.

You could only get but so far, when you moved off hate anyway.

After talking to Jordan that night on the phone, I found out everything that she had said about my mama corroborating the story about me helping her steal people's identities and then snitching on her and getting her time had been a flat-out lie. Jordan had never even spoken to my mama and had paid a columnist, whom had owed her a favor, over at *Gossip Weekly,* to site my mother as a source.

She told me that she had done so because she had wanted to make me look bad on air, for reasons that she couldn't really explain right now. Most likely because she had still wanted Tremaine. She may not have been woman enough to admit to as much at the time, but I knew what it was. He had been with me so therefore, she had come after me. She wanted me out of the way, and this had been her way of accomplishing that task.

All of this over a man.

Well, he was all hers now.

She apologized for being so vindictive and conniving. But her apology didn't mean a damn thing to me at the time because it was too late for me to undo everything that I had done to my mama at her parole board hearing, as a result of the wrongdoing that I'd believed her to have done to me.

That was the reason why you weren't ever supposed to believe anything that you heard in the media, without checking out the facts, first.

I had to live with the things that I had done and hope that my mama would one day, find it in her heart to forgive me for essentially keeping her in prison for five more years, out of spite, which I realized would be a hell of a lot to ask of her.

She would probably never forgive me for what I had done, but I would remain hopeful anyway.

Life was all about karma, good and bad.

You got back what you put out there and it was just that simple.

I couldn't expect her to overlook what I had done, if I wasn't willing to do the same, which was the primary reason why I had decided to give my sisters a pass like I had. Maybe it was too late for me to make amends for the things that I had did and still salvage what was left of my fractured family, or maybe it wasn't.

I didn't know.

But at the end of the day, you couldn't just keep making the same mistakes and expect to get different results.

It didn't work that way.

So, as I turned the chapter on this particular phase of my life and began to set my sights on the things that were to come, I knew that I would do so with an open mind and more, importantly, an open heart. I wouldn't keep score on anybody who I dealt with from this point forward or harbor any feelings of resentment towards them. If I felt that someone who I was involved with couldn't be relied upon, I would distance myself from them and it was just that simple. I now realized that people were going to be people, whether I agreed with the way that they were moving or not.

It was up to me if I chose to deal with them or not.

AUTHOR'S NOTE

Thank you to all who took the time to check out this series and I really hope that it was everything that you were expecting it to be in a series and more. Much, much more. Given the right amount of feedback, you may not have quite heard the last of little miss Seanna. Just putting that out there, right quick. I have a couple of projects in the kitchen right now. Don't know which one that I'll serve up next, but if you follow me, I promise to keep you posted on that. Subscribe to my blog for upcoming releases and *special* discounts.

https://stephenjbrowder.wordpress.com

I told y'all already that I was gonna keep dropping these joints for the whole 2019. Y'all thought I was playing or something? All I ask is that you be gracious enough to bless me with a review on Amazon.

Now, is that too much to ask?

Follow my page on Facebook and become a part of the conversation.

https://www.facebook.com/authorstephenbro wder/

Follow me on Amazon.

https://www.amazon.com/author/stephenbrow der/

Again, I thank you for your time. It's precious and I am extremely humbled by that. I appreciate each and every one of y'all who support me and this dream. A writer only goes as far as their reader's allow them to go. Recognize your power, and I want to thank y'all for even allowing me to get this far because you could've read anyone else's book series in the world, but you chose to read mines. Bump it, hugs for everybody.

Signing off,

Your Friend and Favorite Author,

Stephen J Browder

BONUS CONTENT FROM MY UPCOMING
RELEASE

COMING TO YOU AS A WOMAN

COMING THIS APRIL

CHAPTER 1

RAMONA ARMSTRONG

"You can't be fucking serious right now? Ain't no damn way," I fussed to myself with mounting frustration as I looked at the clock and realized that it was already a quarter after six. I was supposed to be out of the building at five o' clock, along with everyone else who worked at the office.

Dr. Buchanan would probably tear me a new one tomorrow morning, I realized. He had already been on my case about working too much overtime and coming and going as I pleased. He had instructed me to leave when everyone else did and he didn't want to hear any ifs, ands, or buts about it. His words not mine's. But what he failed to realize was that I had a bigger workload than everyone else did with me doubling as the administrative assistant and the front desk clerk, due to the fact, that his ass was too cheap to hire someone else to fill the vacancy, after losing his long-time clerk, Mr. Sheryl, last month to retirement. So really, how fair was that to me when I was taking on so much?

It wasn't like I was riding the clock, just to be riding it.

He really killed me sometimes.

Please.

But besides the petty shit that I had to deal with on occasion, I really loved my job. I had always been someone who got a kick out of interacting with people and not to toot my own horn or anything, but I have been complimented on several occasions for my abilities to get folks to open up to me, when they were trying to be tight-lipped with others.

The Doctor and nurses, especially.

Half the time, I wasn't even aware that I was doing it. It just came natural to me because I was a talker. Blame the Aries in me. I had been this way from about as far back as I could remember and working for an OB-GYN gave me plenty of opportunity to mix it up with other people.

Plus, I was a lesbian, so being around a bunch of women all day, was just an added benefit.

But I'd be remiss if I didn't also point out the fact that I had a lot on my plate and sometimes, it just felt like there weren't enough working hours in the day to get everything done that I needed to get handled. But for some reason, nobody could seem to understand that, so I found myself forever on the defensive about it.

I shut off my computer and packed my briefcase, double-checking to make sure that I hadn't left any documents behind that I needed to look over tonight, like I had the tendency to do at times. Once I was satisfied that I hadn't, I grabbed my keys off the coatrack and proceeded to leave the office.

As I made my way down the hall, I noticed that the door to one of the examination rooms was closed, which was highly unusual because we normally left all the doors wide open when we shut the office down for the day. That way, the rooms would be filtrated properly by allowing the air to circulate throughout it overnight. But for some reason, this one was closed. Assuming this to be just a simple oversight by Mrs. Owens, our chief residential staff supervisor, I turned the knob and pushed the door open, and it was at that point that my life would take a turn that not even I was fully prepared for. Setting off a chain of events that threatened to destroy everything positive that I had going on in my life, which was something that I could ill afford with me being the felon that I was.

It wasn't exactly like I had opportunity beating down my door, so it wasn't wise to squander the few opportunities that I did still have left at my disposal. But sometimes, trouble just sort of had a way of finding you, whether you were looking for it or not.

My jaw dropped to the floor as I gaped at Dr. Buchanan slapping skins with a patient who I had saw, hanging around the office a time or two. A cinnamon-colored woman with weave galore. She wasn't the prettiest specimen in the world with her wide jaw and oversized forehead, but that body of hers had most definitely been blessed by the hands of God. I had never actually dealt with the woman directly or anything, but I had saw her enough times to know that she was the type of chick who was after one thing and one thing only, and that was money. Broads like her didn't care about a relationship or settling down with anyone. For them, the only thing that mattered was how they could capitalize off dealing with whatever unsuspecting fool that they set their sights on, which in this case, turned out to be my boss, Dr. Buchanan.

What a damn fool.

I stared in shock as the good doctor took her roughly from behind. He grinned from ear-to-ear, obviously enjoying the hell out of himself.

"Oooh, Elijah!" the woman called out, citing his first name, while reaching back and spreading her pussy open for him so that he could penetrate a little deeper.

"You love this shit, don't you?" Dr. Buchanan asked, totally absorbed by this woman, which was painful to watch. "Who this miserable ass pussy belong to, huh?"

"You," she said immediately before letting off another series of moans.

"I said who does this pussy belong to?" he asked again but this time, with a lot more conviction.

"It belongs to you!" she shouted at the top of her lungs and shuddered in response.

They both broke wide once the door banged against the wall, alerting them to my untimely intrusion. Their heads snapped in my direction. The woman looked scared. Dr. Buchanan looked aggravated, but I couldn't have cared less right now about whatever it was that he was going through. That was unimportant in my eyes. I stared back at him, refusing to back down, and shook my head in open disapproval as I struggled to make sense of it all.

"How could you do something like this, Elijah?" was all I asked, refusing to give him the respect that his title of doctor called for in this instance, by acknowledging him as such.

I almost caught whiplash as I quickly turned my head away from Dr. Buchanan as he stood before me, bare-assed, without even so much as a warning, and began to put his clothes back on. How rude and inconsiderate. The woman remained on the gurney, where she was wrapped up like a mummy, with the sheets draped around her protectively. The same sheets that we gave our patients, during their exams.

Rotten bitch.

Before I could object, Dr. Buchanan was grabbing me by the arm and guiding me out of the examination room. I tried to snatch away from him, but he was much too big of a man at 5 '10 and about 220, give or take a pound or two, for me to be very effective in that regard.

I was only 5 '2 and a buck and a quarter, at best.

"Get your fucking hands off me," was the only thing that I could say in my own defense as he pulled the door to the exam room, closed, behind himself, blocking the woman off from our conversation. He took his time about releasing my arm from his grasp. I stared at him like he had lost his fucking mind.

"One word of this to anyone and I swear, so help me God, that I will make your life a living hell. Try me if you want to, Ramona. I'm not playing with you, even a l'il bit," he threatened, meaning every word. The worse part about it all was that I knew, more than anybody, that he definitely had the resources available to him to carry out his promise, without even breaking a sweat over it.

I had quite the dilemma on my hands.

Normally, I was the type to stay out of other people's business, at all costs. You could tell me something and I would take it with me to the grave, whether I agreed with it or not. That was just the way that I had been bred. But this was different. A lot different, actually and I didn't yet, know what to do about it.

I realized that bringing him out would more than likely signal the end of my job. The job in which I needed, by the way. But it could also render me homeless as well because the man was also my landlord, so his reach went a lot further than just my occupational interests. Literally, leaving me broke and without a pot to piss in. Literally. Most people wouldn't even consider this as a possibility since the bad so far outweighed the good, but for me, there were other things that I had to consider.

The act in and of itself was so unethical that it was a borderline crime, even. To take advantage of vulnerable women who were trusting you in ways that they had never trusted any other man before and start smashing them, when their defenses were down, was a straight up bitch move, in my opinion. He was a doctor for God's sake, and not just any doctor. An OB-GYN. A women's doctor, and this was the way that he repaid them for giving him that trust?

But for as sickened as I was by this thought, my responsibilities in this thing went even further than that.

I was close to his wife, Janice.

She was a wonderful woman, who deserved a lot better from him than this. In fact, to say that we were close would be a drastic understatement.

She was my best friend in the whole world.

My only friend, in fact.

If it wasn't for her, I would be in a very different place in my life, right about now.

It was her who had bugged her husband for weeks to give me a job at his office, when I had first gotten out of jail, aware that I didn't even have anything that could be remotely considered as a job lead, upon my release. He had expressed reservations about hiring a felon, initially, but she wouldn't quit until he took me on and that was precisely what he did.

It was also her who had convinced him to let me stay in one of his rental apartments, without paying a dime for my first three months, until I got back on my feet, knowing that I had nowhere else to go at the time. Again, he had bent to her will. Janice was such a sweet woman that it was very hard to turn her down about anything. Not that she ever asked for much. But once she did, you better be prepared to carry out whatever task that she needed you to because you wouldn't be able to turn her down, so why waste time trying to in the first place? Unless you were just a glutton for punishment. The woman was an angel on Earth, and she had always gone above and beyond for me, which was why I owed it to her to shed some light on the devilish deeds of her cocky, unappreciative clown of a husband.

I mean, what type of friend would I be, if I didn't?

There was only one little problem, though.

I knew that she would never believe it, in a million years.

Even coming from me.

Made in the USA
Coppell, TX
13 October 2020